EVERY SECRET LEADS TO ANOTHER

# SECRETS *of the* MANOR

Kay's Story, 1934

BY
**ADELE WHITBY**

Simon Spotlight
New York   London   Toronto   Sydney   New Delhi

Kay
Wilson

Alfie
Vandermeer

Joseph
Wilson

Kate
Vandermeer
Wilson

Katie
Vandermeer
Goodwin

William
Vandermeer

Eleanor
Wakefield
Vandermeer

Kathy
Vandermeer
Spencer

John
Vandermeer

Sally
Jameson
Vandermeer

Alfred
Vandermeer

Katherine
Chatswood
Vandermeer

Mary
Chatswood

The Chatswood

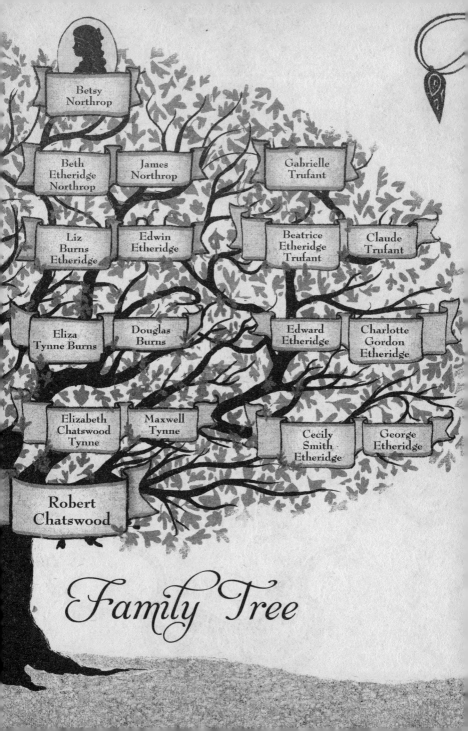

Betsy Northrop

Beth Etheridge Northrop

James Northrop

Gabrielle Trufant

Liz Burns Etheridge

Edwin Etheridge

Beatrice Etheridge Trufant

Claude Trufant

Eliza Tynne Burns

Douglas Burns

Edward Etheridge

Charlotte Gordon Etheridge

Elizabeth Chatswood Tynne

Maxwell Tynne

Cecily Smith Etheridge

George Etheridge

Robert Chatswood

*Family Tree*

SIMON SPOTLIGHT
An imprint of Simon & Schuster Children's Publishing Division
1230 Avenue of the Americas, New York, New York 10020
This Simon Spotlight paperback edition January 2015
Copyright © 2015 by Simon and Schuster, Inc. Text by Ellie O'Ryan.
Illustrations by Jaime Zollars. All rights reserved, including the right of
reproduction in whole or in part in any form. SIMON SPOTLIGHT and
colophon are registered trademarks of Simon & Schuster, Inc. For information
about special discounts for bulk purchases, please contact Simon & Schuster
Special Sales at 1-866-506-1949 or business@simonandschuster.com.
Designed by Laura Roode. The text of this book was set in Adobe Caslon Pro.
Manufactured in the United States of America 1214 OFF
2 4 6 8 10 9 7 5 3 1
ISBN 978-1-4814-2756-2 (hc)
ISBN 978-1-4814-2755-5 (pbk)
ISBN 978-1-4814-2757-9 (eBook)
Library of Congress Control Number 2014935642

Betsy!" I cried, waving my arm wildly in the air. "Betsy! Down here!" Ever since the enormous steamship had pulled into Boston Harbor, I'd been craning my neck in hopes of catching a glimpse of my cousin, Betsy Northrop, and her mother, Beth Etheridge-Northrop. At last, the passengers had begun to disembark—and a good thing, too, because I couldn't wait another moment to finally meet Betsy and Aunt Beth!

Mom slipped her arm around my shoulder, pulling me into a hug that made me stop waving. "I can't wait to see them either, Kay," she said. "But there's no way Betsy can hear you—or even see you—all the way down here. We'll just have to be patient for a little longer. I'm sure she and Beth will walk down the ramp as soon as they can."

I smiled sheepishly as I leaned my head on Mom's shoulder. I knew she was right, of course, and I knew that it really wasn't proper for me to make such a spectacle of myself, waving and shouting on the docks. But patience had never come easily to me—especially not now of all times, when meeting Cousin Betsy was just moments away!

For years, we'd planned to visit Chatswood Manor in England for Betsy's twelfth birthday. Not only would it be my very first trip overseas, but I'd finally get to meet my English relatives, and even attend Betsy's spectacular twelfth birthday ball. Most intriguing of all, Mom and Aunt Beth had promised to tell Betsy and me a long-held family secret on Betsy's birthday. For months, Betsy and I had written letters back and forth, trying to guess what it could be, since Mom and Aunt Beth wouldn't give us a single clue.

But all our plans had unraveled six weeks ago, when Mom and Dad were on the brink of losing everything—including our home, Vandermeer Manor, which had been in the family for generations. Our situation was so dire that Mom and Dad had no choice but to cancel the trip, as well as my twelfth birthday ball. It was such a terrible disappointment that I felt like I'd been on the brink of tears for weeks. But I always choked them back. If Mom and Dad could stay optimistic despite everything we'd lost, then so could I.

From across the ocean, Aunt Beth and Betsy were determined to help us. Not only did Betsy cancel her own birthday ball in solidarity, but they made arrangements to come to America to celebrate *my* twelfth birthday instead, which was just four days away. When I read the news in Betsy's letter, I was amazed. It was an act of kindness I knew I'd never forget.

"Kay! I see them!" Mom cried. She pointed to the ramp, and even though I'd never met Betsy and Aunt Beth before, I recognized them at once from the photograph on Mom's bureau: beautiful Aunt Beth, her gorgeous red hair gleaming in the summer sun, and Betsy following behind her, looking like a smaller copy of her mother.

"And there's Nellie!" Mom said as she recognized her former lady's maid.

At that moment, Aunt Beth spotted Mom; I could tell because she stopped suddenly and, leaning over to say something to Betsy, pointed in our direction.

When Betsy looked at me, our eyes locked for a long, wonderful moment, which needed no words at all.

Then Betsy stood on her tiptoes and started to wave.

"Hi, Betsy! I see you!" I yelled, completely forgetting Mom's advice as I jumped up and down to wave back. I glanced at Mom—and realized that she was waving and jumping up and down, too!

"Go on, you two," Dad said, laughing. "I'll catch up."

Mom and I hurried through the crowd to the base of the ramp, where we waited eagerly for Aunt Beth and Betsy to set foot on solid ground after five days at sea.

At last, they did!

"You're here!" I cried. "You're finally here!" And then Betsy and I were hugging and laughing and our mothers were crying happy tears as they embraced, and it felt like nothing in the world would ever be wrong again.

I stood back to get a better look at my cousin. Right away, I noticed that something was missing.

"Betsy, where is it?" I asked. "Where is the Elizabeth necklace?"

She glanced quickly at her mother. "Mum said I shouldn't wear it so prominently while we were traveling. It's in my trunk. And that's not all—"

"Betsy," Aunt Beth said in a surprisingly stern voice.

Betsy ducked her head. "Right. I know," she said quietly.

*Know what?* I wondered. It was like Betsy and Aunt Beth were speaking in code. I was about to ask Betsy what she meant when she smiled at me—almost apologetically—and shook her head, leaving me even more confused.

"Well, I can't wait to see it when we get home," I finally said. I'd heard lots of stories about the Elizabeth necklace. Just like the Katherine necklace that Mom used to wear every day, the Elizabeth necklace was the stuff of family legend. Long ago, our great-great-grandmothers, twins named Elizabeth and Katherine Chatswood, had received the precious necklaces for their twelfth birthday. Like the twins themselves, the necklaces were almost identical: a golden pendant in the shape of half a heart, which hung from a delicate chain. Each necklace glittered with gems in the girls' favorite colors: sparkling red rubies for Katherine and shimmering blue sapphires for Elizabeth. The twins' mother, Lady Mary, had selected the necklaces herself for their twelfth birthday. Sadly, Great-Great-Great-Grandmother Mary had died before Katherine and Elizabeth's birthday. The necklaces were her very last gift to her daughters, which made Elizabeth and Katherine cherish them all the more.

The twins never took off their special necklaces, not even on their wedding days. As the older twin, Elizabeth was destined to marry her cousin Maxwell Tynne and live her days as the lady of Chatswood Manor in England. Katherine's life had charted a very different course when she married another distant cousin, Alfred Vandermeer, and immigrated to America. As the decades passed, the necklaces had grown even more precious to our families as they were presented to the firstborn daughter of each generation on her twelfth birthday. From Great-Great-Grandmother Katherine to Great-Great-Aunt Kathy to Great-Aunt Katie to my own mother, Kate, the tradition had continued, growing stronger with every passing year.

But not this year. Not for me.

It was still hard to believe sometimes that it wasn't all a terrible dream, part of the long nightmare we'd been living ever since my parents told me that we'd lost control of Vandermeer Steel, the company my great-great-grandfather Alfred had founded. One by one, the familiar parts of my life had started slipping away—first most of the staff had been let go; then we'd moved out of Vandermeer Manor and into the groundskeeper's cottage; and then, to our shock, Dad had pawned the Katherine necklace to make an urgent payment that kept Vandermeer Manor out of fore-closure. The money from the Katherine necklace had saved Vandermeer Manor . . . for now, at least. Though we couldn't afford to live there anymore, Mom and Dad had decided to open the house for tours and rent-als. The extra income from rental fees could've been used to buy back the Katherine necklace. But someone else had bought it first . . . and now it was gone forever.

I'd never forget the night that Mom found out what Dad had done. I'd heard upset words—from both of them—followed by hours of crying. By the next day, though, Mom had forgiven him. And I couldn't stay mad at Dad, either. Not when he worked so hard, each and every day, to save our family from ruin. There was nothing I wouldn't sacrifice for our family, and I knew that Mom and Dad felt the same way. I would've sold my art supplies and my collection of movie magazines in a heartbeat if they'd been worth anything.

"If you ladies will excuse me, I'll go see about the trunks," Dad was saying.

Mom squeezed his hand before he left. Then she turned to me. "Kay, I'd like you to meet someone. This is Nellie."

"It's an honor to meet you, Miss Kay," Nellie said as she dropped into a curtsy.

"Oh, Nellie, you don't have to do that!" I exclaimed as I took her hand. "I've heard so much about you—Mom's been missing you for years and years, and Shannon and Hank, well, they sing your praises all the time! Taking Shannon's place in England all those years ago so she could stay here after she fell in love with Hank is just about the most noble, most selfless—"

Nellie flushed with pleasure. "Miss Kay, you speak too well of me."

"Come along. The car is this way," Mom said.

"You can sit next to me," I promised Betsy as we

walked toward the car. Dad soon joined us, followed by a porter who was pushing a heavy cart piled high with luggage.

"Five trunks, correct?" Dad asked Aunt Beth.

She nodded. "Yes, thank you, Joseph."

Dad grinned at her. "One of these days, you're going to have to start calling me Joe," he said as the porter began to load the trunks into our car. "After all, we've been family for almost fifteen years."

After Dad tipped the porter, he held open the back door for us. "Next stop, Vandermeer Manor," he announced.

Betsy glanced around. "Where's Hank?" she asked.

"He's at work," Mom told her. "You'll meet him later."

"Work?" Aunt Beth asked.

"Yes. He's a foreman for Vandermeer Steel now," Dad replied. "We had some good luck when a position opened up at the same time we realized that we couldn't keep Hank on as a chauffeur anymore."

"Then who will drive us home?" Betsy asked, looking confused.

Dad made a funny bow. "Yours truly, Betsy. I'm at your service!"

Mom and I laughed at Dad's silliness, and after a moment Aunt Beth and Betsy joined in, too. But a faint blush had crept into Betsy's cheeks. I wanted to reach out and squeeze her hand. *Don't be embarrassed!* I'd say. *It was an honest mistake. How were you supposed to know that Dad would be driving when you've always had a chauffeur?*

Then I noticed the look Aunt Beth was giving Betsy. I knew that look. I'd seen it plenty of times on Mom's face.

It meant: *Be careful.*

And that made me feel embarrassed, too. Embarrassed that Aunt Beth and Betsy were so sensitive to our hard times that they felt like they had to walk on eggshells around us, minding every word they said.

I ducked into the car. "Sit here, Betsy!" I said, pretending I hadn't noticed anything.

"I can't wait to see Vandermeer Manor," she said as she climbed in after me.

"Nor can I," Aunt Beth agreed. "After all these years, it will feel like coming home again."

The drive back to Bridgeport, Rhode Island, wasn't

too long—only a couple of hours. When we were nearly there, Dad turned off the main road.

"Just a brief stop," he called over his shoulder as he pulled into a filling station. We waited in the car as he pumped the gas, whistling a cheerful tune under the watchful eye of the attendant. But I wasn't feeling very cheerful inside. *What must Aunt Beth and Betsy think of Dad pumping his own gas?* I wondered. But if they were concerned, they didn't let on.

"Won't be long now," Dad said when he got back into the car. He took a sharp turn onto Miller's Pond Lane, a dusty road that traveled right by Memorial Park. Not so long ago, the flat, grassy field had been a place of quiet reflection, dotted with statues and tributes to soldiers who had fallen during the Great War. But in the last few years, Memorial Park had transformed into a Hooverville—a shantytown, named for President Herbert Hoover's failure to stop the Great Depression. Tattered boards and boxes had sprung up like weeds. They were a poor excuse for houses, but they were better than nothing—which was all that many people had left.

Aunt Beth peered out the window, a frown of

confusion on her face. "Who are those people?" she asked. "What are they doing there?"

"They're the unluckiest of us all," Mom replied. "They've lost their homes and their livelihoods and have made shelters to live in as best they can."

Betsy's mouth dropped open. "They *live* there?" she said with sorrow in her voice. "In boxes?"

Aunt Beth reached for Betsy's hand. "It's such a shock to see," she said to Mom. "We've read about your country's struggles in the papers, of course—but they haven't done justice to the level of suffering."

"You shouldn't have come this way," Mom murmured to Dad.

"I didn't have a choice, Kate," he replied in a low voice. "The other route is longer, and we can't afford the extra fuel."

Aunt Beth stared out the window as if she hadn't heard them, but of course she had. Every word. I snuck a glance at my cousin's face and saw that she, too, was looking out the window. After a few more agonizing minutes, we left Memorial Park behind, though I knew that it was still present in everyone's minds.

Dad was the first to break the silence. "Better times

are on the way, thanks to President Roosevelt's New Deal," he said.

"I'm glad to hear you say that," Aunt Beth said. "I'd like to hear more about this New Deal, Joseph. Does it contain any provisions to help Vandermeer Steel?"

Dad sighed. "Well . . . yes and no," he said. "It's a little complicated. I'll tell you all about it at dinner, Beth. As you can see, we're just about home, and I'm sure you and Betsy and Nellie will want to—"

"Is that it?" Betsy suddenly cried, leaning toward the window. "Is that Vandermeer Manor?"

A sense of pride surged inside me at my cousin's reaction to my family's home, the place where I'd been born, the place where I'd lived my entire life. "Yes," I told her. "We're almost there."

"It's beautiful," Betsy breathed. "So grand! So stately!"

"I'm happy to see it again," Aunt Beth said, smiling as she gazed up at the tall gables. "Those few days I spent here when I was a girl were some of the happiest of my life."

"And mine, too," Mom said.

Betsy and I grinned at each other, and I knew that

we were thinking the exact same thing: What would happen to *us* during her visit, to fill us with the same sort of wonderful memories that Mom and Aunt Beth shared?

I could hardly wait to find out!

We continued down the long, graceful drive that led to the main house of Vandermeer Manor. But before we reached the paved circle in front, Dad turned onto a side road instead. I still wasn't used to making that turn. I wasn't sure that I ever would be.

A few minutes later, Dad parked next to the groundskeeper's cottage—or what *had been* the groundskeeper's cottage. Now it was our home. And standing right in front of the little cottage were Shannon and her two children, Clara and David. I smiled when I saw them assembled there, just like they would have stood in front of the great house to welcome visitors. It made me feel like some things were the same, even though so much had changed.

"Here we are!" Mom said cheerfully as Dad opened the door for us.

"Lady Beth!" Shannon cried. "Welcome back!" In an instant, they were hugging and crying as the happy reunions continued. Then Shannon turned to my cousin. "This must be Lady Betsy, of course. What a thrill to meet you at last!"

As Shannon started to curtsy, Betsy rushed up to hug her instead. "It's an honor to meet you, Shannon!" she said. "Mum's told me so much about you!"

For a moment, Shannon looked surprised; then her face broke into a wide smile. "Such a sweet lamb, and so grown-up already! Where have the years gone?"

"I'm sure I don't know," Aunt Beth said, laughing.

"I'd like you to meet my children, Clara and David," Shannon said.

Clara stepped forward to curtsy to Aunt Beth and Betsy. Clara was almost grown-up, already sixteen years old, which made her feel like a big sister and a friend rolled into one. David was fun, too, even though he was much younger than me. I could never feel sad or lonely when Shannon and Hank's kids were around.

"Kay's told me all about you in her letters," Betsy said to Clara. "I feel as though I already know you."

"It's an honor to meet you, Lady Betsy," Clara replied. "Really and truly!"

"Would you like to go inside?" Mom asked Aunt Beth.

"Yes, I'd love to see your new home," she replied. In the entryway, Aunt Beth paused and nodded approvingly at the brand-new telephone stand, which was all her doing. After the telephone in Vandermeer Manor was disconnected, Aunt Beth took it upon herself to make arrangements for a new phone line to be installed in the cottage.

"This is the living room," Mom explained as the whole group followed her inside. "It's like a parlor and a sitting room and a study combined. The dining room is over there—it's very convenient, actually, to have it connected to the kitchen. The food is always piping hot since it doesn't have to travel all the way upstairs."

"Yes, that would be convenient," Aunt Beth agreed. "What a charming home you've made, Kate."

But I had to wonder if Aunt Beth was really being honest . . . or just being nice. The cottage suddenly felt tight and cramped with all of us crowded together in the entryway. Compared to how Aunt Beth and Betsy lived at Chatswood Manor, it must've seemed more like a playhouse than a real house to them.

"We have three bedrooms—Beth, I thought you could take the green one, and, Betsy, you'll share a room with Kay, if that's okay with you," Mom continued.

"Just like we did, twenty years ago!" Aunt Beth laughed.

"I'd *love* that," Betsy said enthusiastically. "It will be so much fun. Like an adventure!"

"Where are Great-Aunt Kathy and Aunt Katie?" Aunt Beth asked, glancing around.

"They're in New York," Dad replied. "They'll oversee the sale of the town house and finish packing up the last of our belongings there."

Once again, I saw a pointed look pass between Aunt Beth and Betsy, but I didn't understand what it meant.

"I suppose we should rest a bit before dinner," Aunt Beth said, still looking at Betsy.

*Does Betsy* really *want to rest?* I wondered. I couldn't wait for the chance to sneak away with her so we could talk privately, just the two of us. And I was dying to see the Elizabeth necklace! I decided to follow Aunt Beth and Betsy to the bedrooms, but before I could join them, I heard Mom call my name. I turned around to see her standing in the doorway to the kitchen, holding out my apron.

"Shall we start dinner?" she asked.

By the time Aunt Beth and Betsy emerged from their rooms, the table was set and dinner was ready to be served. Mom had planned a fancy meal to welcome our relatives. The small table was crowded with bowls of fresh rolls, green beans, buttered carrots, and mashed potatoes. There was even a platter of pot roast, a dish that Shannon had just recently taught us how to cook.

"Everything looks wonderful!" Betsy exclaimed. "I could smell it cooking in my room!"

I smiled at her, but inside I was mortified. In the tiny cottage, you really could smell kitchen odors in every room. Such a thing would never happen in Vandermeer Manor.

As soon as everyone was seated, Mom began to serve the food, piling each plate high. I shifted nervously in my seat. Mom and I hadn't been cooking for very long—just a few months. What if dinner was an inedible disaster? Or even just passably good? I already knew that Aunt Beth and Betsy wouldn't complain, even though they were used to eating all their meals prepared by a professional chef. But that only meant that their standards would be higher.

Luckily, I was worried for no reason.

"*Mmm*, delicious," Betsy said after her first bite. "And you cooked it all yourself? Every dish?"

"We did indeed," Mom said proudly.

"That's astonishing," Betsy marveled. "I wouldn't even know where to begin. Would you, Mum?"

Aunt Beth shook her head. "I'm afraid I've never cooked a meal in my life," she said. "That seems like a shameful thing to say, but it's true."

"Neither had I, a few months ago," Mom replied.

"You're all so clever," Betsy continued. "Driving your own car, cooking your own food. It's really something!"

"Yes," I said awkwardly. Mom and Dad insisted there was no shame to living in reduced circumstances, but Betsy's fuss embarrassed me all the same.

Aunt Beth dabbed at her mouth with her napkin. "If I might change the topic of conversation," she began, "I'd like to ask about Vandermeer Steel. Specifically, how can we help?"

There was a pause while Mom and Dad looked at each other across the table.

"Come, come," Aunt Beth continued gently. "We're all family. There must be no secrets between us. Betsy and I are here to do whatever we can to assist you."

"That's a generous offer, Beth, and we thank you wholeheartedly," Dad finally said. "And if we could accept your generosity, we would. But I'm afraid that it's not so simple."

"I understand," Aunt Beth replied, though she sounded like she didn't understand at all. "Well, perhaps you might explain everything from the start, and then we can all put our heads together and see if we can't find a way forward."

"I'm sure you remember that when Father died, my brother, Alfie, inherited the company, and I inherited the estate," Mom spoke up. "Alfie is . . . many things, but a shrewd businessman he is not."

"He transferred a great deal of Vandermeer Steel's capital to the stock market, thinking he could make a fast buck," Dad explained. "But when the crash happened, all the money disappeared. It was gone in an instant."

"How devastating," murmured Aunt Beth.

Mom nodded sadly. "Then, as things got worse, Alfie began selling shares of Vandermeer Steel to foreign investors so that he would avoid destitution," she continued. "I tell you, Beth, I miss Mother every day, but I'm very glad she did not live to see Alfie make such terrible decisions. And, of course, last year, Alfie ran off. We don't know where he's hiding, but Vandermeer Steel is in our hands now. We can be thankful for that, at least."

"As a result of Alfie's decisions, we're no longer in control of Vandermeer Steel, but are beholden to these foreign investors until we can raise enough capital to buy back the shares," Dad said. "Without a strong cash flow, we've had a devil of a time securing contracts for new construction. We're the lame duck of the building industry."

Aunt Beth's face suddenly brightened. "What about that New Deal?" she suggested. "I thought I read that there were programs specifically designed to help struggling companies. If you had the capital to begin new construction, then you'd surely start to turn a profit again."

Dad smiled ruefully. "Yes, you're right about that," he said. "The only problem is that Vandermeer Steel is not an American company at the moment. As long as foreign investors hold a majority share—"

"And I suppose I couldn't just buy them out," Aunt Beth mused, "since I'm not an American, either."

"Exactly."

For a long moment, no one spoke. At last, Aunt Beth said, "Well, this is a conundrum."

"I have faith that we'll turn things around for Vandermeer Steel in time," Mom said, always looking on the bright side. "The more pressing problem is the debt to—"

"Kate," Dad said suddenly. He looked pained. "Must we?"

"It's all right, Joseph. Joe," Aunt Beth said, quickly correcting herself. "You mustn't be embarrassed."

"We have a sizable payment due on a debt in four days," Mom continued, giving Dad an apologetic look.

*The same day as my birthday,* I thought, but I didn't say it.

"If we default on the payment, we'll lose Vandermeer Manor," Mom said.

"That mustn't happen," Aunt Beth said right away. "Here, at the very least, let me make the payment for you—"

"Really, that won't be necessary," Dad said firmly. I could see the gleam of pride shining in his eyes. "I have an important meeting in Providence with an old friend, Randall Roberts. He's whip smart and not one to let a tremendous investment opportunity pass him by. I'm confident that I'll be able to secure enough capital from Randall to make the payment on time."

"And if not, we'll find something else to sell," added Mom. "The valuable jewelry is gone, of course, but there are still antiques in the manor house."

Again, no one spoke, and I could tell that we were all thinking of the Katherine necklace. If I were completely honest, if I dug deep down into my secret-most heart, I could admit how sad I was that I'd never have the chance to wear it, or even see it again. But I'd never do that to Dad. He felt bad enough.

I glanced at Betsy, hoping to see her Elizabeth necklace. Two things surprised me right away: the fact that she still wasn't wearing it and the look on her face. It was hard to describe, a mixture of urgency and importance, as though there was something serious she had to say. And she was staring at Aunt Beth, who—strangely enough—was shaking her head *no* at Betsy.

*Is this all about the Katherine necklace?* I thought. Maybe Betsy wasn't wearing the Elizabeth necklace because she felt so bad for me. How could I tell her that I wouldn't mind a bit if she wore her Elizabeth necklace? That I *wanted* to see her wearing it?

"Hopefully, it won't come to that," Aunt Beth said. "There are still four days, after all." Then she smiled at me. "And I know something else important that happens in four days!"

"Have you made any special plans for your birthday?" Betsy asked.

"All that matters to me is that we have cake, and that Betsy and I finally learn the truth of the Chatswood family secret you have been promising to tell us," I announced, making everyone laugh. "I already got my present—a visit from the best aunt and cousin a girl could hope for!"

"Our celebrations might not be fancy, but we'll make a nice day of it," Mom promised. "A picnic on the beach, perhaps? Or maybe we could drive into Providence and see a movie! How would you like that, Kay?"

"Go to the movies? All of us?" I said excitedly. It had been so long since I'd seen a movie—what a treat that would be! "I read in *Hollywood Hello* that Paul O. Brady's new movie just premiered. His movies are some of my favorites!"

"All of us," Dad echoed. Then he reached for my hand. "I'm so sorry about the Katherine necklace, sweetheart. I'll never be able to apologize enough—"

"No, Dad. I'm glad it could be put to good use," I interrupted him.

"And now that we're here, you must put us to good use as well," Aunt Beth said. "We've not come to be pampered and petted, but to work. We'll clean, we'll cook—we might be terrible dolts in the kitchen, but we'll do our best. Whatever must be done, just say the word. Right, Betsy?"

"Right, Mum," she replied, but that same troubled look had settled over her face.

And then, in an instant, I realized what the problem was. Cleaning, cooking . . . Betsy didn't want to do those things—and why would she? I could hardly blame her. I knew what it was like to live in a house full of servants, whose entire existence revolved around meeting my every need. It was very different from how we were living now.

And she wanted no part of it.

3

*I* could tell I'd overslept as soon as I woke up the next morning; the sun was already shining brightly through the yellow-checked curtains. Betsy and I had stayed up so late the night before that Mom and Aunt Beth had come in *three* times to tell us to go to sleep, but we just couldn't stop chatting and giggling. Mom and Aunt Beth weren't really upset with us, though, since they were doing the same thing in the living room!

I rubbed my eyes sleepily as I glanced over at Betsy's bed. Though it was empty, the sheets and blankets were all tangled up. *Maybe Betsy didn't want to wake me up by making her bed,* I thought. But more likely, it had never even occurred to her to make the bed. I'd never made my own bed until a few months ago.

*I'll do it for her,* I thought suddenly as I pushed

back my blanket. *That will make her feel like she's back at Chatswood Manor.*

As I smoothed Betsy's sheets, I realized that I could hear a pair of voices through the wall. It was Aunt Beth and Betsy—and it sounded like they were arguing!

I froze, straining my ears to listen. But it was hard to make out what they were saying.

Very slowly, and without making a sound, I crept onto the bed and pressed my ear against the wall. It was easier to hear them now—a little easier, anyway.

"Mum, you don't understand—*something-something-something*—I can't stand—*something-something!*"

"What makes you think I don't *something-something*—"

"It's *something-something* awful to—"

"I agree, but you know we can't—*something-something*—until her birthday. And not a moment before."

"It's not fair!"

I turned away from the wall, feeling sick and ashamed—and not just because I'd been eavesdropping, something Mom and Dad had always taught me not to do. Was Betsy really so miserable in our little cottage that she couldn't stand it here? Was Aunt Beth forcing her to stay until my birthday so that my feelings wouldn't be hurt?

*If that's the case, they should just go,* I thought numbly. *There's no reason for them to suffer just for me.*

I continued making Betsy's bed, lost in my thoughts, until the door creaked open.

"Oh, good! You're awake," Betsy said in a surprisingly chipper voice. "Aunt Kate told me to fetch you for breakfast. What are you doing?"

I turned away to give the pillow one last fluff—and also to avoid looking at her. "I was just making your bed."

"You goose! You don't have to do that!" Betsy scolded me, laughing. "Tomorrow you must show me how to do it, all right? Then I'll be able to make it myself."

"If you want," I said, trying to sound normal. But even I could tell that my voice was strained.

After I got dressed, Betsy and I went to the dining room, where Mom had placed a platter of waffles on the table beside a pitcher of fresh-squeezed orange juice. She really was doing everything she could to give Aunt Beth and Betsy a nice visit. I hoped that somehow, some way, Betsy would realize that. It would break Mom's heart to know how much Betsy wanted to leave.

We were nearly finished with breakfast when Aunt Beth suddenly clapped her hands together. "Now, in all our discussions last night, we failed to talk about something *very* important," she announced. "Kay and Betsy's birthday ball!"

I gasped in surprise. Mom hesitantly put down her cup of coffee. "Now, Beth, I know you phoned before you left England and said you wanted to pay for a joint birthday ball for both girls, but I'm not sure. We can't help with the cost and—"

Aunt Beth cut my mom off. "I am well aware of that and it's my decision. If we start planning now and send invitations to our friends and relations overseas by the end of the week, we could have the ball next month."

Despite herself, Mom's face brightened. "Beth, you are too generous, and I'm afraid I'm simply too excited by the prospect of a birthday ball to argue with you."

Aunt Beth clapped in delight. "Wonderful. Then it's settled. I will deal with invitations and all other details, but tell me, have you spoken to your dressmaker about new gowns?"

"I'm afraid we don't employ a dressmaker anymore," Mom admitted as her smile faded. "I don't need a new dress, and—"

"Of course you do," Aunt Beth said firmly. "You mustn't worry about the expense, Kate. This is a gift from me to you."

"I have a lovely gown from before the Depression that will be fine," Mom replied. "And Shannon has offered to help me add new trim so that it won't look out of fashion. I want Kay to have a birthday gown, though. It seems only right."

"No," I spoke up, shaking my head. "No, Mom. I don't need one." A birthday ball gown that I'd wear only once was way too frivolous an expense, even if Aunt Beth had offered to pay for it.

But my words only made Mom's frown deepen. "Kay, you should have a new dress," she said in a quiet voice. "It's important to me."

There was an uncomfortable silence around the table as I tried to figure out what to say. If it meant so much to Mom—and if it was a gift from Aunt Beth—I should probably just give in. But even as I tried to convince myself to have a new dress made, a small voice in my mind repeated, *too expensive, too expensive, too expensive.*

"What about a ready-made gown?" Betsy spoke up. Everyone turned to look at her.

"When we went to London just before my birthday, we saw ever so many charming gowns in the shops," she continued. "They were all the latest fashion, too. And I don't think they're quite so expensive as a custom gown from a dressmaker."

"No, Betsy, they aren't," Mom said, smiling again. "That's a fantastic idea! What do you think, Kay? Would you like to go to shopping in Providence for a birthday dress?"

"Sure." I finally gave in. "But only if we can all go."

"I wouldn't have it any other way," Aunt Beth replied.

"I'm off to Providence tomorrow for my meeting with Randall. We can drive in together." Dad took one last sip of his coffee before he rose from the table. "I'll be home at the usual time today," he said as he kissed Mom's cheek.

"Dinner will be waiting," she told him. Then Mom turned to me. "Kay, would you like to show Betsy around the grounds? She might enjoy seeing the gardens and the cliffs."

"Will we go to the sea?" Betsy asked excitedly. "I've brought my bathing costume."

I glanced out the window at the gray clouds that had appeared while we were eating. "It looks like it might rain, so we'd better stay close to home," I said. "But we'll go to the beach another day, Betsy. Promise."

After we cleared the breakfast dishes from the table, Betsy and I got our umbrellas and went outside.

"Where should we go first?" I said. "There's the rose garden, and the shade garden, and—"

"Might we start at the cliffs?" Betsy asked. "They sound so magnificent."

"Sure," I replied. "You're not afraid of heights, are you?"

"No," Betsy said, but she didn't look convinced. "At least, I don't think so."

"It's okay. There's a railing so you won't fall over the edge," I told her.

As we walked through the meadow toward the cliffs, Betsy linked her arm through mine. "I feel like I should pinch myself, Kay!" she exclaimed. "It's hard to believe that this is real."

"I know exactly what you mean," I told her. "I've been daydreaming about meeting you for my entire life—and now you're finally here!"

"Can you believe my mum made this same trip to meet your mum, twenty years ago?" Betsy asked. "No wonder she wanted to hide when my grandparents insisted that she come home early. I'd try to hide, too, if something happened to cut my visit short."

*Would you?* I wondered. But all I said was, "Here we are."

For a moment, Betsy was speechless. "Oh, Kay," she whispered. "It's stunning."

I looked toward the ocean, where the wild sea churned. The clouds were moving quickly toward us, and the wind was starting to pick up. Mom and Dad had always warned me that the cliffs were no place to visit during a storm. Not only were the rocky trails slippery when it rained, but the high winds made the narrow path even more dangerous.

"We should get back," I said. "I think it's going to rain soon."

"I hate to leave," Betsy said, still staring at the white-capped waves. "This is one of the most beautiful places I've ever been."

"We'll come back," I promised her. "On a fine, sunny day, when the wind isn't so strong."

"All right," Betsy finally agreed. But as we turned to leave, something caught her eye. "Kay, isn't that Clara?"

I glanced over and saw Shannon's daughter sitting on a bench. "What's she doing here?" I said in surprise.

"Let's go find out," Betsy said, a note of determination in her voice.

We hurried toward the bench. "Clara!" I called. "Clara! A storm's coming. Shouldn't we—"

Clara scrambled to her feet and dabbed her eyes with a handkerchief. But there was no hiding the fact that she'd been crying.

"What's wrong?" I asked in concern.

Clara waved her hand in the air, as if her problems were no more bothersome than a pesky fly. "Oh, it's nothing I should trouble you with, Miss Kay," she replied. Then she glanced at the horizon. "I believe you're right about that storm, though. We should go back."

"Walk with us," I said. Clara smiled a bit as she fell into step between Betsy and me, but I could tell that something was troubling her.

"Won't you tell me what's wrong?" I asked Clara. "I'd like to help if I can. And so would Betsy, I'm sure."

"Of course I would!" my cousin said.

"It's a silly thing to be upset about," Clara said, looking a bit embarrassed, "but . . . the thing is . . . I've been offered a job."

"A job!" I repeated. "Well, that's—I mean—well! That's really something!" I couldn't imagine why Clara was upset at such a prospect, so I didn't want to say something that might upset her more.

"Congratulations!" Betsy said enthusiastically. "What sort of work is it?"

Clara tried to smile, but couldn't quite manage it. "Mrs. Morgan has requested my services as a lady's maid," she said. "The letter came in the morning mail, and Mom and I've been arguing ever since it arrived."

"Don't the Morgans live in Boston?" I asked.

"Yes," Clara replied.

"And you don't want to go?" Betsy asked gently.

Clara shook her head. "It's good work," she said,

as if she were trying to convince herself. "Respectable. And Mrs. Morgan is a kind woman. But—this sounds so foolish I'm ashamed to say it—I don't *want* to be a lady's maid!"

"Clara's a great one for arithmetic," I told Betsy. "She can do all sorts of figures in her head. Dad used to call her the Human Abacus when she was little."

"Mr. Wilson promised me a job in the accounting office when times are better," Clara continued sadly. "I had an apprenticeship there last summer and it was wonderful! I'd much rather work for Vandermeer Steel than Mrs. Morgan."

"I know Dad will keep his promise," I said.

"I'm sure he will," Clara replied. "But Mom's insisting that I take the job with Mrs. Morgan! She says a real job today is better than the hope of a job tomorrow. Plus, she says it's time for me to do my part . . . and I suppose she's right. I'm old enough to have a job and send money home, just like she did when she went to work at Chatswood Manor."

I bit my lip as I tried to figure out how to respond. Everything that Shannon had said about the situation made sense, but it seemed so unfair for Clara to take a job she didn't want! Not to mention that the thought of her moving away made me feel like I was about to cry. I could hardly imagine life at Vandermeer Manor without Clara.

"Poor Clara," Betsy said sympathetically. "It's so dreadful to disagree with your mother. Mum and I had a really awful time of it this spring and it made me miserable."

Clara looked at her with gratitude. "That's exactly it!" she exclaimed as her eyes welled up with tears again. "Mom's always been my greatest ally—about everything, really. But now . . . I can't imagine that we'll ever see eye to eye on this. It feels like she wants to send me away!"

"No," I said firmly. "I know that's not the case, Clara. Shannon loves you more than anyone."

"Then why won't she *listen* to me?" Clara said. "I don't want to go!"

"And I don't want you to," I replied.

"It's tricky, isn't it?" Betsy said thoughtfully. "There's such a fine line between following your heart and fulfilling your duty to your family."

"Great-Great-Grandmother Katherine came to

America for love *and* duty," I said. "But I bet even she was scared to leave Chatswood Manor."

"And just look at all she built here," Betsy added, gesturing to the beautiful manor house before us. "A dynasty of her very own!"

No one spoke, but I was sure we were all thinking the same thing: a dynasty slipping away from us more and more every day.

"That's a good way to look at it," Clara finally said. "We never know what kind of opportunity waits just around the corner."

"When do you have to decide?" I asked.

"Mrs. Morgan would like me to start next week," Clara told me.

"Next week!" Betsy exclaimed in surprise. Then she caught herself. "I mean, anything could happen between now and then. Don't give up hope, Clara!"

At last, Clara smiled. "Thank you, Lady Betsy. You've said just what I needed to hear." Then she leaned over to hug me. "I'm so grateful, Kay. Thanks for listening."

"I'll talk to Mom and Dad," I told her. "If there's *anything* we can do—"

But Clara shook her head. "No. Please don't bother them with my little problem," she replied. "I know Mr. Wilson would make good on his promise if he could."

A rumble of thunder sounded in the distance, so we quickly parted ways—Clara hurrying in one direction to the cottage where she lived and Betsy and I hurrying in the other.

Betsy stopped abruptly. "There's something I forgot to tell Clara," she said. "I'll be right back, Kay."

"I'll come with you," I offered.

"No, no, I'll just be a minute," Betsy told me. Then she was off like a flash.

I watched Betsy run after Clara, who was nearly halfway home. Clara leaned her head close to Betsy while Betsy whispered something in her ear. Then an enormous grin filled Clara's face.

*What* are *they talking about?* I wondered. So many different emotions swirled in me that I didn't know what to do with them all. It had never occurred to me before that Clara might leave us. Knowing just how smart she was, Dad had always said that there would be a place for her at Vandermeer Steel.

But a lot had changed since then—and the future

was more uncertain than ever before. Not just for the family business and our home, but for me, too, I realized. Because if things *didn't* turn around—if Dad wasn't able to pay off his debts and regain control of Vandermeer Steel—I'd be in Clara's situation before too long. What sort of jobs would be available to someone like me?

Just then, there was an enormous clap of thunder that seemed to shake the cliffs, and the rain began pouring down. My hair and dress were drenched before I could even open my umbrella.

"Betsy!" I called through the storm. "Hurry!"

She held up one finger as she finished saying something to Clara. Then Betsy dashed toward me through the pelting rain.

"I'm soaking wet!" Betsy shrieked gleefully.

"What were you and Clara talking about?" I asked as we ran home.

Betsy shook her head. "Very sorry, Kay, but I can't tell you," she replied. "I'm sworn to secrecy."

"Sworn to secrecy?" I repeated, surprised. Betsy and Clara had just met, and already they were friendly enough to have secrets? Secrets from *me*?

"My lips are zipped," Betsy said solemnly. Then she started giggling. "Isn't that a funny phrase? I'd never heard it before Clara said it! She's great fun, isn't she? I can already tell that Clara and I will be fast friends. Maybe she can come over tonight after dinner!"

"Maybe," I echoed as I tried to figure out why I felt a pang of jealousy. A friendship between two of my favorite people in the whole world was a good thing— something that should make me happy.

So why did I suddenly feel so sad?

4

$\mathcal{T}$he next morning, everyone was in a giddy mood as we drove to Providence. Dad was so optimistic about his business meeting that he even whistled on the way!

"I'll be back to pick you up at two o'clock," Dad said when he dropped us off in front of Gladding's Department Store. "Be ready to celebrate!"

"Give my regards to Randall. I know you'll do wonderfully," Mom told him, and they shared one of their special smiles that they saved only for each other. It always made me happy to see them smile like that.

"My! What an enormous shop!" Aunt Beth marveled.

"It's actually three stores," I corrected her. "This is Gladding's, and that's Shepard's over there, and that one is called Cherry and Webb. See the covered bridge up there? That's so you can shop at all three stores in poor weather without getting wet."

"Outside of New York, you won't find a better place to shop on the Eastern Seaboard," Mom said. "Let's go straight to the fourth floor—that's where we'll find formal gowns for Kay."

"And then you can lead us to wherever we might find formal gowns for you," Aunt Beth said. "Because we're not leaving here until you've picked out a dress. Isn't that right, Kay?"

"Right!" I said, grinning. I'd never heard anybody tell Mom what to do before.

"What sort of dress do you want?" Betsy asked me as we stepped into the elevator. "Have you thought much about the color or style?"

"Not really," I said slowly. "I always thought my dress would be red, to match the Katherine necklace. But I suppose that doesn't matter now."

"Oh, no, Kay, you should still wear red!" Betsy said right away. "It's . . . That's a Vandermeer tradition, isn't it?"

"I suppose. But green is awfully flattering on me."

"No. We'll look for a *red* dress for you," Betsy said firmly. "Like Mum always says, tradition is important."

"My mom says that too!" I said as I burst out laughing.

"Fourth floor," the elevator operator announced. "Good day, ladies."

We stepped off the elevator into an elegant world of shiny satin, stiff taffeta, and lustrous silk. Every gown seemed more glamorous than the one before, the sort of things that movie stars would wear to a Hollywood premiere.

"Oh, gracious!" I exclaimed. "How will I ever choose?"

"That's what we're here for," Betsy told me. Then she pulled me into the sea of dresses. "Come on, Kay! Let's find the prettiest dress in the shop!"

I couldn't begin to count how many dresses I tried on that day. They were all lovely—some were stunning, even—but each one had some small flaw that was hard to overlook. One was too short, another too long; one too tight in the waist and another too loose. As soon as we decided against one dress, Betsy would dash off in search of another to take its place.

"We really should've brought Shannon or Nellie," Mom said, shaking her head. "They'd have a better idea about which alterations we could easily make on our own."

"There must be a seamstress employed here," Aunt Beth said, glancing around. "Where's the shopgirl? I'll ask."

"No, Beth, we shouldn't spend—"

"Nonsense," Aunt Beth said. "Whatever it takes to fit Kay with a dress that makes her feel like a princess."

"We just haven't found it yet," Betsy said to me, trying to sound reassuring even though she looked as disappointed as I felt. "Let's keep looking."

By that point, we'd circled the dress department three different times. "This one fits the best," I said, holding out a simple maroon dress. "It's just a little too long. And I'm sure Shannon can help me hem it."

Betsy shook her head. "It's so plain, though," she replied. "Hardly any trim at all! I still think we can find you a prettier gown, Kay. I'll be right back."

"What do you think, Mom?" I asked. "Is it too plain?"

She gave me a lopsided kind of smile. "No, sweetheart, not at all," she said. "A girl as beautiful as you doesn't need embellishments on a dress to make her shine."

I blushed happily at the compliment.

"Kay!" Betsy said, all out of breath as she ran up to me. She thrust a cherry-red gown in my direction. "I've found it. I've found it! I've found your dress!"

"Where'd you spot this?" I asked.

"It was buried back there," she replied. "I think it's the only one left in that color. Oh, do try it on, Kay! You're going to look so gorgeous!"

As I ducked back into the fitting room, I tried not to get my hopes up. Other dresses had seemed perfect, too—until I tried them on. Then they just left me disappointed.

But that didn't happen this time.

The satin dress had a scalloped skirt that looked like it was made of rose petals, with fluttery sleeves trimmed with lace. My favorite part was the hundreds of tiny seed pearls sewn on the bodice in an intricate swirl. And best of all, the dress fit as though it had been made just for me!

I stepped out of the fitting room, where Mom, Betsy, and Aunt Beth were waiting for me. Then I did a little twirl.

"Oh, Kay," Mom said in a soft voice as a beaming

smile crossed her face. "You look wonderful."

"Positively lovely!" Aunt Beth added. "It suits you perfectly."

"Oh, I knew it would!" Betsy said gleefully. "Do you like it, Kay?"

"Betsy, I love it!" I spun around again. "I wish I didn't have to take it off!"

Everyone laughed, and then Aunt Beth said, "But you must, I'm afraid, so that we can find some accessories to go with it. Perhaps an ornament for your hair, and new shoes, and a new pair of gloves—"

"No, Beth, that won't be necessary," Mom spoke up. "You've already been far too generous."

Aunt Beth frowned a little. "It's nothing, Kate."

"I already have gloves, Aunt Beth," I told her. "They're practically new. And I'm sure we can find enough accessories at home for me to wear."

"If you're sure I can't change your mind," Aunt Beth offered one more time. I shook my head firmly in response.

"Very well, then." She sighed. Then she turned to Mom. "All right, Kate. It's your turn."

"No, no," Mom said. "This is *Kay's* shopping trip."

Betsy and I exchanged a glance. I reached into the fitting room to get the one dress I hadn't tried on . . . the one dress that Betsy and I had hidden there, anticipating this very moment. It was made of raspberry-pink silk woven with gold threads, and I had a feeling it would be perfect for Mom . . . if we could convince her to try it on.

Mom knew what I was up to, of course. She gave me a pointed look.

"Please, Mom, won't you try it on?" I asked. "Just so we can see it?"

"Oh, all right," Mom said as she stepped into the fitting room. When she emerged a few moments later, I could tell from the gleam in her eyes that she'd fallen in love with her dress as quickly as I'd fallen in love with mine.

Aunt Beth took one look at Mom and said, "Kate, I won't take no for an answer. It's a stunning gown and you look marvelous in it."

"It *is* a lovely dress, isn't it?" Mom said thoughtfully, rubbing the delicate silk between her fingers. "Very well made, too."

"You look so pretty, Aunt Kate," Betsy said. "Oh, do get it! You must!"

"Then we'll all have new dresses to wear to the ball, Mom," I added. "Won't that be special?"

For a moment, Mom looked torn. Then a grin spread across her face. "All right, all right," she said, throwing up her hands. "I give in. I'll get the dress!"

Betsy and I cheered as Aunt Beth started clapping. Dad had told us to be ready to celebrate when he picked us up, and that's exactly what we felt like doing!

Then Mom hugged Aunt Beth. "Thank you for the wonderful gifts you've given Kay and me today. Your generosity has touched my heart."

By the time Aunt Beth had settled the bill and the clerk had wrapped up the dresses in two large boxes, it was time for lunch, so Aunt Beth treated us to a meal at Shepard's Tea Room. I couldn't remember the last time I'd eaten out at a restaurant. It was such an elegant affair, with gold-edged china, crystal goblets of lemonade, and a small army of forks and spoons. I breathed a sigh of relief when I remembered which fork to use for each course! Everything seemed so much brighter and happier with Aunt Beth and Betsy; we laughed and laughed and had such a nice meal that we lost track of the time and were nearly late to meet

Dad. All four of us were still laughing when we hurried back to Gladding's, where Dad was waiting for us.

One look at his face, and our laughter stopped on the spot.

"What do we have here?" he asked in a lighthearted way, nodding toward the packages. "I see that Gladding's was good to you!" But his eyes were sad, and there was a discouraged slump to his shoulders.

Mom rested her hand on his arm. "Did Randall . . . ?" she began, a hopeful edge to her voice.

Dad smiled at her, but the sorrow didn't leave his eyes. "Afraid not, my dear. But tomorrow will be a new day, and each new day brings new hope."

A troubled look passed between Aunt Beth and Betsy, but Mom's shoulders straightened; if she was disappointed by the news, she'd never show it. "How right you are, Joe," she said. "We'll find a way. We always do."

"Aunt Beth bought us the prettiest gowns, Dad." I spoke up, hoping to recapture the cheerful mood.

"That's wonderful, Kay," Dad replied, sounding distracted. "Just wonderful. We're in your debt, Beth. Thank you."

"No thanks necessary," Aunt Beth replied quietly.

We got into the car and began the drive back to Bridgeport. But unlike our morning drive to Providence, a heavy silence had settled over everyone. There was no more excited chatter or hopeful laughter. In fact, no one even spoke until we were nearly home again.

"Do we have another trip scheduled to Providence?" Mom said abruptly.

"I guess we'll go back in two days for my birthday movie," I replied. "Why?"

Mom stared out the window. "We'll make an extra stop at Gladding's so I can return that dress. I don't need it. It's an unnecessary extravagance. I don't know what I was thinking."

"Kate," Aunt Beth said. "I *want* you to have it."

But Mom just shook her head. "No, Beth, no. It would be bad enough for me to waste my family's money. It's shameful for me to waste yours."

Mom continued staring out the window, but I could see the tight, pinched look on her face in the reflection. It was all my fault—I'd pushed and pushed her to buy the dress, and now the thought of owning it filled her with regret. But it wasn't fair for Mom to go without any nice things.

None of it was fair.

"It's not a waste!" I cried. "You looked beautiful in it, and it made you so happy!"

Mom finally turned to look at me. "You know, Kay, I don't think it was the dress that made me happy. It was the fun I was having with you and Betsy and Aunt Beth. The shopping and the fancy luncheon—those things were delightful, of course—but what really made it special was being with some of my favorite people in the world."

"And there's no reason for our jolly times to end just because we've left Providence," Aunt Beth said smoothly. "I have an idea. What if we spend the rest of the day inside Vandermeer Manor? I'd very much like to see the grand rooms again, and perhaps we might begin preparing the house for tours. What do you say, Kate?"

The worry on Mom's face seemed to melt away. "That would be wonderful, Beth," she said. "There's so much to do. And it always makes me feel better to see progress made."

"That's why Betsy and I are here," Aunt Beth said as she patted Mom's hand. "Whatever we can do, we're at your service!"

"Would you like me to drop you off at the main house, then?" Dad asked.

"Yes," Mom said firmly. "We'll get started right away!"

Mom unlocked Vandermeer Manor's great oak doors with her brass key. Then the four of us stepped inside the front hall.

"Since no one's living here at the moment, we keep the drapes drawn so that the furniture and carpets won't fade," Mom said. "But Shannon, Kay, and I come in every week to dust."

Aunt Beth sucked in her breath sharply. "It's as beautiful as I remembered," she whispered. "One of the grandest homes I've ever seen."

I understood why Aunt Beth was whispering; such a solemn, quiet air had settled over Vandermeer Manor that it seemed important not to disturb it. Back when we had lived in the house, it had been full of activity: servants bustling from room to room, deliveries of groceries and supplies, and an endless stream of visitors. Now, in the silence, I couldn't tell if the house was lonely . . . or simply resting. I wondered if Vandermeer Manor missed us as much as we missed living here.

*It's just a house, Kay,* I scolded myself. *It* can't *miss us.*

But was it just a house? As Mom drew back the heavy velvet drapes at each window, sunlight poured into the rooms, sparkling off the crystal chandeliers and gleaming on the polished marble floors. My ancestors had designed Vandermeer Manor, and each room still boasted Great-Great-Grandmother Katherine's touches—from the faceted doorknobs to the portraits that hung on the walls. How could Vandermeer Manor ever be just a house, when our lives had unfolded here for generations? That mattered, didn't it? That had to count for something.

*But now it's time for a new chapter,* I reminded myself. *A new adventure is about to begin. For us, and for Vandermeer Manor, too.*

An easy calm had settled over Mom now that she was back in Vandermeer Manor. *Mom lived here more than twice as long as me,* I realized. *She must miss it even more than I do.*

"Would you like a tour, sweetheart?" Mom asked Betsy.

"Would I ever!" Betsy exclaimed. "I can't believe I'm standing inside Vandermeer Manor. It's more beautiful than I imagined."

"I apologize that some of the rooms are a little bare," Mom explained. "Like the library—you'll see that several shelves are empty. We sold some of the rare books a few months ago."

Aunt Beth nodded understandingly. "Rare books can fetch a tidy sum," she said. "Though I'm sure it broke your heart to part with them."

Mom paused. "Well . . . yes and no," she said. "I would've grieved if they'd been lost in a fire. But I can't be too sad, knowing that they're safe and sound in the possession of someone who will appreciate and enjoy them as much as we did."

"That's a wise way to look at it," said Aunt Beth.

"All my life, I've placed a great importance on the things around us," Mom continued. "As if it were the things themselves that contained my happy memories or favorite moments. If there's one bit of good that's come out of this ordeal, it's that I've seen the error of my ways." She held her arms out. "It was never the things that mattered, really. It was the people who used them. Letting go of the things doesn't mean that we're letting go of the people we loved."

"Have you emptied Katherine's rooms?" Aunt Beth asked.

"No, I'm not quite ready for that," Mom replied with a laugh. "When I visit Katherine's rooms and see everything just so—just the way she left it—it's like I can still feel her presence. I miss her so much."

Then Mom turned to Betsy and me. "But I was thinking that you two might be able to sort through Essie Bridges's old rooms in the East Wing," she said.

For years, the East Wing had hidden one of the biggest secrets of Vandermeer Manor: Essie Bridges, who had been Katherine and Elizabeth's lady's maid when the twins were girls. Essie had accompanied Great-Great-Grandmother Katherine to America to be her lady's maid after she married. But when Essie developed a devastating sensitivity to the sun that made it impossible for her to go outside without breaking out in a painful rash, Katherine had moved her into the East Wing and cared for her until Essie had passed away, several years before I was born.

"Sure," I told Mom.

"What exactly do you want us to do?" asked Betsy. I glanced at her out of the corner of my eye. From her tone of voice, I couldn't tell if she was unhappy about the work ahead of us—but she didn't look upset.

"Let's talk about it on the way," Mom said as she led us toward the main staircase. "Our first step will be sorting through everything to organize it—so you'll dedicate one area for papers, another for clothing, a third for books, and so on. After everything has been sorted, you can help Aunt Beth and me decide what should be done with it."

"Oh, Kate, look," Aunt Beth suddenly said. "The alcove! After all these years—it hasn't changed a bit!"

"No, it hasn't," Mom said with a smile.

"Is this *the* alcove?" Betsy asked. "Where you put your necklaces together and said Elizabeth and Katherine's special chant?"

"The very same," Aunt Beth said. "It was the day before Kate's birthday—"

"I'd just received the Katherine necklace at tea," Mom remembered. "The Great War was looming, and Beth's parents had insisted she return home right away."

"How wise they were," Aunt Beth said, "though of course we didn't know it at the time. We were so young back then, remember, Kate? We had a whole scheme planned for me to hide in the East Wing! But there was great danger for ships crossing the Atlantic Ocean during those dark days, even for passenger vessels."

"It was a terrible time," Mom said, shaking her head.

"We stood right here," Aunt Beth continued as she walked over to the tiny alcove off the East Wing, "and we said the chant we'd read about in Essie Bridges's journal. 'I am Beth, and I love my cousin Kate.'"

"'I am Kate, and I love my cousin Beth,'" Mom said.

"Forever!" they said at the same time.

"Then we put the Elizabeth and Katherine necklaces together to make a whole heart—" Aunt Beth said.

"It was the first time they'd been together in nearly sixty years," Mom interrupted her.

"And they made a funny little noise, and then—*pop!*—a tiny door in the back of each pendant snapped open!" Aunt Beth finished. "All these little slips of paper tumbled to the floor."

"When I unscrambled them, I thought they spelled out 'apart forever,'" Mom said. "It was heartbreaking! But Great-Grandmother Katherine told me that some of the letters were still stuck in our necklaces, and that the message really said 'a part of you forever.'"

Mom paused to unlock the entrance to the East Wing. "We'll be in the study if you need us."

Entering the East Wing was like stepping through a time machine; nothing in it had been disturbed since before Betsy and I had even been born. The three rooms—a sitting room, a bedroom, and a powder room—were filled with a lifetime's worth of knick-knacks and mementos.

"Goodness," Betsy finally said. "I hardly know where to begin."

"It's best to start in one little corner," I told her, glad to share what I'd learned from sorting through other rooms. "We could tackle the writing desk first, I guess."

"That sounds like a good plan," Betsy agreed. "It's probably full of papers and curios."

Betsy was right. Each drawer contained stacks of letters that were tied with satin ribbons. I slipped a yellowed letter from one stack and began to read it. "'29 November, 1827. Dear Clarice, I am writing to you in great haste with news that you will find surprising—perhaps even shocking.'"

I stopped reading abruptly. "It's not right to read this," I said. "It's someone else's correspondence. I feel like a snoop."

"But it was written in 1827," Betsy pointed out. "That's more than a hundred years ago! Clarice and the letter writer are dead and buried by now, whoever they were."

"Still," I insisted as I slipped the letter back into its packet. "We'll just make a stack for all the papers and let our mothers decide what to do with them."

"As you wish," Betsy agreed. "Oh, look, Kay, how lovely! It's got to be Katherine and Elizabeth!"

I peeked over her shoulder at the daguerreotype in her hands. "You look like them," I said.

Betsy started to laugh. "That's funny—I was just thinking the same about you!"

"Ooh, what's that?" I asked as I reached past Betsy

to a shiny object. It was circular, with sections of metal twisted and turned around each other to form an endless loop. A small arrow protruded from one end. The beautiful object dangled from red and blue ribbons that had been woven together.

"That's called a Celtic knot," Betsy said knowledgeably. "It's a symbol of Ireland. Funny, though—it almost looks like a key."

"Or a necklace," I said, holding it up by the ribbons. "It would be a pretty thing to wear. I'll start a curio pile."

"Why don't we put the curios on that empty bookshelf?" Betsy suggested. "That might help keep things orderly in here."

"Great idea," I replied. "Actually, Betsy, why don't we move all the books down to the library? We'll be able to fill the empty shelves down there while making room up here for organizing."

"Perfect!"

Betsy and I each scooped up an armful of books and set off for the library. "I suppose we should make sure that Mom approves of this idea," I said. "Let's stop by the study first."

We found Mom and Aunt Beth sorting through an enormous stack of old invoices. "I'm not sure now why we ever held on to all of these," Mom was saying. "What possible use could I have for a grocery bill from 1917?"

"Hello, darlings," Aunt Beth said as we walked into the room. "What have you brought us?"

I told Mom and Aunt Beth about our plan. "Is that all right?"

"It's fine with me," Mom replied.

Aunt Beth rose from her chair and crossed the room. "I adore old books," she said as she took one from the stack in my arms. "The softness of the pages . . . the cracked leather binding . . . even the smell! I love wondering about who might have read them before, or finding a forgotten bookmark. An old book is like a mystery and a puzzle all rolled into one."

She gently opened the book. "'*Bleak House*. A novel by Charles Dickens,'" she read from the title page. "Oh, that's one of my favorites! And look here—see the date? 1853. This must be a first edition."

"I have some Dickens books as well," Betsy said. "*The Adventures of Oliver Twist. A Christmas Carol . . .*"

"*David Copperfield. The Life and Adventures of Nicholas Nickleby*," I added, reading the titles of the other books in my arms.

"There's a mark in this one," Mom said as she, too, began flipping through one of the books.

We crowded around Mom to examine the pair of swirly letters that had been written inside the front cover.

"This one, too," I said.

"And mine as well," Aunt Beth spoke up. "And this one . . . and this one . . . and this one . . . ," she said as she checked each book. "What does that look like to you?"

"The first letter is certainly a C," Mom said. "I'm not sure about the second. We don't have anyone in the Vandermeer line whose first name begins with a C, though."

"I had a grandmother Charlotte and a great-grand-mother Cecily," Aunt Beth said. "But I can't imagine how their books would've ended up in Essie Bridges's possession in Vandermeer Manor."

Betsy squinted at the letters scrawled in her book. Suddenly, her face grew pale, and the book fell to the floor with a loud *thud*. We all jumped from the sound.

"Betsy!" Aunt Beth said anxiously. "What's wrong?"

Betsy's hands were shaking as she picked up the book. "It's a *D!*" she exclaimed, her words tumbling out in a rush. "*C.D.* Charles Dickens!"

The silence surrounding us was electric. The expression on Mom's face kept shifting, from disbelief to shock to astonishment to . . . Was that hope?

"Were there other books like these?" Aunt Beth asked in a low, urgent voice.

I nodded, feeling tongue-tied.

"Run and fetch them please, girls," she told us.

Betsy and I ran as fast as we could to the East Wing.

"Do you think—?" she said, all out of breath as we piled the rest of the Dickens books into our arms.

"I don't know," I replied.

Then we were off again, racing through the hallways so fast that we couldn't spare a second to talk about the amazing discovery.

While we were gone, Mom and Aunt Beth opened every other Dickens volume to reveal the same initials in each book.

C.D.

C.D.

C.D. C.D. C.D.

Mom bit her lip anxiously, still too cautious to give in to her hope. "I just don't know enough about rare books to be sure," she said.

"Kate," Aunt Beth replied, her eyes shining with happiness, "it's entirely possible that there were first editions of Charles Dickens books, initialed by the author, in the Chatswood library. We know that Katherine brought many things from home with her when she emigrated . . . and if these books were among them . . ."

"And if she loaned them to Essie . . . ," Mom began, then covered her mouth with her hand. She looked like she was about to cry.

"I can't begin to imagine what they would be worth," Aunt Beth replied. "First editions of some of the most famous novels ever to have been written, initialed by the author. Priceless, really, to the right collector."

"It's like Great-Grandmother Katherine is *still* providing for her family!" Mom exclaimed. "I've got to call Vivian—she's been handling all the sales of Vandermeer antiques. Beth, do you realize what this might mean? If the books really are that valuable . . . we'll be able to pay off the debt!"

"Go!" Aunt Beth laughed as she gave Mom a gentle push toward the door. "Telephone Vivian at once! Don't delay a moment!"

Mom laughed, too, as she kissed each of us in turn. Then she hurried out of the study to use the phone back at our cottage.

I was so happy that I felt like dancing. "Oh, Aunt Beth, how much do you think they'll sell for?" I said. "Could it be enough that we'll be able to buy back all the shares of Vandermeer Steel, too?"

Aunt Beth put her arm around me. "I doubt they're worth quite that much, darling," she said, a cautious edge to her voice. "And we don't know for certain that the books really were signed by Dickens."

Betsy frowned. "But, Mum, what *else* could it be?" she argued. "There haven't been any C.D.s in the family!"

"There will be time enough for celebrating if these initials are proven to belong to Charles Dickens," Aunt Beth said. "Please try to keep your expectations in check. I'd hate for you to be disappointed if we're wrong."

"I understand, Aunt Beth," I replied. But secretly, in my heart, I agreed with Betsy.

What else could the initials possibly mean?

6

$\mathcal{T}$he next morning, Betsy and I were in the middle of a race to see who could make her bed first when Mom knocked on the door.

"Kay, could I have a word with you in my bedroom?" she asked.

"Just a minute!" I said as I rushed to smooth out the blanket. All I had to do was fluff my pillow and—

"Done!" Betsy shrieked before she dissolved into giggles. She flopped onto her freshly made bed. "I win!"

"Did not!" I joked. "See? My bed is neat as a pin, but your blanket's all wrinkled since you climbed on it!"

Betsy leaped off and smoothed out her blanket once more. "Maybe so . . . but you have to admit that I *did* finish first."

"Kay," Mom said to remind me that she was waiting.

"Sorry!" I said right away. I followed Mom to her

room, where she closed the door behind us. "Is everything all right?"

"Yes, of course," she replied as she sat on the edge of the bed. She patted the blanket, so I sat next to her. "Tomorrow's the big day . . . your twelfth birthday!"

"I can't believe it," I replied. "It almost doesn't feel real."

"Dad looked up show times in the *Providence Journal*," Mom told me. "That movie you've wanted to see is playing at—"

"Actually, I changed my mind," I said quickly. Even though I really, really wanted to see Paul O. Brady's new movie, I was worried that a trip to Providence would give Mom the chance to return her dress. "Why don't we have a picnic on the beach instead? Betsy brought her bathing suit and she's really eager to spend a day at the shore."

Mom looked surprised. "Are you sure that's what you want?"

I nodded emphatically. "Positive."

"Then that's what we'll do," Mom decided. "You know, when Beth visited me twenty years ago, she wanted to go to the shore as well, but we didn't have the chance when her trip was cut short. She'll be just as excited as Betsy."

I grinned. Knowing that made me even happier that I'd decided to change our plans.

"There's something I'd like to show you," Mom said. She reached into her bedside table and withdrew a small velvet pouch. "Hold out your hands, sweetheart."

I cupped my palms together and held them out toward Mom, wondering what she was going to place in them.

A mischievous smile crossed her face. "Now close your eyes."

As soon as my eyes were closed, I felt several small objects fall into my hands. When I opened my eyes, I gasped. There were a dozen stars cupped within my palms!

Of course, they weren't real stars, but star-shaped hair ornaments, each one attached to a narrow hairpin. The most amazing thing was the way they shimmered, catching and reflecting the light whenever they moved.

"Do you like them?" Mom asked almost shyly. "I wore them in my hair when I married Dad. Hardly anyone knew they were there besides Shannon and me; my veil was so full that it completely hid them."

"They're beautiful," I told her. "So shiny and shimmery!"

"They're made from mother-of-pearl," Mom explained. "It was important to me to wear something from the sea on my wedding day. I had the Katherine necklace, of course, which connected me to my English heritage, but I also wanted something that would reflect my heritage as a daughter of the Rhode Island cliffs."

We were quiet for a moment before Mom continued. "I confess, Kay, that I still find it hard to believe that I won't be giving you the Katherine necklace tomorrow."

"Mom, it's fine," I began. But she wouldn't let me finish.

"It's *not* fine," Mom told me. "Not at all. You've been very brave in how you've handled such a bitter disappointment, Kay. Some girls your age would've pouted and sulked and made Dad feel even worse about it. But not you. The Chatswood in you has never shined brighter, my sweet girl."

"What do you mean?"

"These are trying times in which we live. Yet you've made sacrifices without complaint, adjusted all your expectations about how your life would be, and somehow, despite all the setbacks, you've managed to maintain a sunny disposition. I can't begin to tell you how much hope and strength Dad and I have drawn from your example."

I shook my head in confusion. Mom had it backward. Didn't she know that *she* was the one who stayed hopeful and optimistic, no matter what we encountered? That *she* was the one setting the good example for the rest of us?

"Dad and I won't stop looking for the Katherine necklace, Kay," Mom continued. "And if we ever have the chance to buy it back and return it to its rightful owner—that's you, of course—we will. And until that day comes, we'll just have to start a new family tradition instead, won't we?"

"Like what?" I asked, still fiddling with the pearlescent stars in my palm.

"Like my wedding stars, perhaps," Mom said. She brushed my hair away from my face and deftly pinned it in place with the stars until they formed a twinkling constellation in my hair. "I'm not sure how fashionable they are these days, but if you'd like them, dear heart, they're yours."

I smiled up at her. "I'd *love* them," I replied happily. "They're so beautiful, Mom. Thank you! And . . . when I have a daughter someday . . . I'll give them to her, too. A new tradition for future Katherines."

Mom kissed my cheek. "Nothing in the world would've pleased your great-great-grandmother more," she said.

There was a knock at the door. "Kate?" Aunt Beth called. "There's a woman here to see you."

"I'll be right there," Mom called back.

I followed Mom to the front door and recognized our visitor right away. It was Mrs. Vivian Lynch, the antiques dealer.

"Vivian, welcome," Mom said as she held open the door. "I'd like to present my cousin, Lady Beth Etheridge-Northrop of Chatswood Manor, England."

Mrs. Lynch looked startled for a moment, but she quickly regained her composure. "An honor to meet you, Lady Beth."

"And you as well," Aunt Beth replied warmly.

"May I offer you something to drink?" Mom asked. "Kay, run and put the kettle on—"

Mrs. Lynch clapped her hands together. "Oh, Kate, you're an impeccable hostess, but what I have to tell you simply can't wait!"

Mom raised her eyebrows in surprise. "Goodness! In that case, please have a seat."

After we sat down in the living room, all eyes turned to Mrs. Lynch.

"I received a phone call late last night from a *very* important buyer," she said dramatically. "He was calling to inquire if I had anything new from Vandermeer Manor—"

Then Mrs. Lynch paused to glance at Aunt Beth. "I'm known in the antiques world for my special relationship with the Vandermeers," she explained. "Buyers come to me for the very best pieces from the Vandermeer collection."

"And was there anything in particular that this buyer was looking for?" asked Mom.

Mrs. Lynch smiled coyly. "I told him about the find you made yesterday—first editions of several titles by Charles Dickens," she replied. "And I mentioned that they *may* have been initialed by the author. Well, Kate, brace yourself, because he made—on the spot!—a *very* generous offer."

Aunt Beth and I leaned forward expectantly, but Mom sat as still as a statue. "How generous?" she asked in a low voice.

"He offered to buy them *sight unseen!*" Mrs. Lynch continued. "Now, I'll tell you, Kate, that's rare. That doesn't happen every day. And I told him, well, I don't know for certain that they were initialed by Charles Dickens himself. I haven't had them verified yet. But he didn't even care! He said his offer stands regardless of the authenticity of the initials!"

"How generous?" Mom repeated.

Mrs. Lynch reached into her pocketbook and withdrew a folded piece of paper. She held it out to Mom without speaking. As Mom reached for the paper, I noticed that her hands were trembling. She unfolded the paper without making a sound, and her dark brown eyes darted back and forth as she read the number written there. When Mom glanced up again, it was impossible to interpret the look on her face.

"Who is this buyer?" she asked abruptly. "Is this offer legitimate?"

"Oh, yes, I've worked with him for years," Mrs. Lynch said. "He's based on the West Coast, but is in New York right now on business for POB Enterprises, which has a particular interest in English and Irish pieces. If you'd like my advice, I say take it, Kate. Make the sale. Honestly, I think this is an outlandish sum, far more than the books are worth, but as they say, a fool and his money are soon parted. If POB Enterprises is willing to pay this amount for books that haven't been verified, then by all means, let them!"

Mom blinked a few times, as if she were having trouble believing what she was hearing. "And this offer—is firm?" she asked. "It's not contingent on financing or verification or—"

"If you're ready to sell, I can have the money in your account by tomorrow morning," Mrs. Lynch told her.

"Very well, Vivian," Mom said. "I'd be happy to sell the books to POB Enterprises."

"Excellent!" replied Mrs. Lynch. "I saw the telephone stand in the entryway—if you don't mind, I'd like to place a few calls."

"Be my guest," Mom said.

"I'll let POB Enterprises know that you've accepted the offer, and I'll telephone my assistant to meet me at the manor house with some crates and packing material," Mrs. Lynch continued. "We'll have the deal concluded by dinnertime."

"Wonderful news, Vivian. Thank you," Mom said, beaming.

As soon as Mrs. Lynch was out of earshot, I pounced. "How much, Mom?" I asked, forgetting that it was rude to discuss money so openly. "How much for the books?"

"Enough to pay the debt that's due tomorrow, *plus* enough to buy back some shares of Vandermeer Steel stock!" she whispered ecstatically.

Despite myself, I began jumping up and down with excitement and even let out a happy squeal.

"Oh, Kate, I'm so happy for you!" Aunt Beth exclaimed as she wrapped Mom in a hug. "You were right. Katherine really *is* looking out for you!"

Suddenly, I glanced around and realized that Betsy wasn't with us. *Maybe she's reading,* I thought. I slipped away to check my bedroom, but Betsy wasn't there.

"Aunt Beth, do you know where Betsy is?" I asked, when I returned to the living room.

"She went out for a walk," Aunt Beth replied. "I'm sure she'll be back soon."

But that wasn't good enough. If I didn't tell Betsy the big news, I felt like I might burst! And I couldn't wait to show her the star hair clips Mom had given me. "I'll go look for her," I said as I took my straw hat off the rack.

Outside, the day seemed even more beautiful now that it had been brightened by Mrs. Lynch's announcement. *Imagine the look on Dad's face when we tell him!* I thought, practically skipping down the path. *He won't believe it! After worrying so much about how we'd ever pay off that debt before it came due . . . and just think of it, the answer to the problem was hiding in Vandermeer Manor all along.*

I paused as I glanced around me. The grounds were especially quiet, since it was the gardener's day off. Betsy could've been anywhere. I decided to stop by Hank and Shannon's cottage in case Clara or David had seen her.

There were two turns in the path that led to Shannon's house, and it wound so close to the cliffs that I could hear the waves crashing below. *After I find Betsy, we've got to get back to our sorting in Vandermeer Manor,* I thought, determined. *Who knows what other treasures we might find? Maybe something even more valuable—something that could pay for more shares of Vandermeer Steel! And then we could move back into Vandermeer Manor and Dad could hire Clara and Mrs. Lynch might be able to track down the Katherine necklace and we could buy it back and—*

As I approached Shannon's house, I heard something else: the sound of laughter, carried on the ocean breeze. I had found my cousin. She was right inside the door, laughing with Clara like they'd been best friends for years.

I quickly ducked behind a lilac bush so they wouldn't see me. Through the blossoms, I watched them; Clara, her face full of smiles as she told Betsy something, and then Betsy, practically doubled over from laughter. I swallowed hard. It wasn't jealousy exactly, but something else that made my throat feel so small and tight.

*If Betsy wanted to visit Clara, why didn't she wait for me?* I wondered. *I would've come with her. We all could've had fun together.*

But that's not how it happened. Instead, it was the two of them on the inside, laughing like they didn't have a care in the world.

And me, on the outside, looking in.

Alone.

7

The very next day, my twelfth birthday arrived at last! *Today, I am twelve,* I thought as I scrambled out of bed. Since Betsy was already gone—she seemed to get up earlier every day—I stared at my reflection in the mirror. I looked the same, but I sure felt different. Not exactly older or wiser . . . but ready, I guess, to face whatever the future might hold—starting with the family secret that Mom and Aunt Beth would finally reveal today.

There was a quiet knock, and the door opened just enough for Betsy to peek in. Her whole face brightened when she saw me. "Happy birthday, Kay!" Betsy cried as she rushed into the room, wrapping me in a lilac-scented hug.

"Thank you!" I said, laughing as Betsy filled my arms with flowers. "What's all this?"

"The lilacs growing near Shannon's house are the best I've ever seen," she explained. "She let me pick some for your special day."

*Did Clara help?* I wondered. But I quickly pushed the thought from my mind. I was twelve years old now, and it was time to put petty jealousies behind me.

After I got dressed, Betsy and I went to the dining room for breakfast. Our parents were already there.

"The birthday girl!" Aunt Beth exclaimed.

Mom and Dad hugged me at the same time.

"Happy birthday, Kay," Mom said as she kissed my forehead. "I love you so much."

"And so do I," Dad added. "Happy birthday! I'm sorry I can't come with you to the beach today. I'm headed to Providence to pay off that debt. Then I'll use the rest of the money to buy as many shares of Vandermeer Steel as I can."

"That's okay, Dad," I said. "We'll have even more to celebrate at dinner tonight!"

After breakfast, Betsy, Aunt Beth, Mom, and I got ready to spend the whole day at the shore. I'd been spending days at the beach my whole life, but I never had as much fun as I did with Betsy. I showed her how to build a sand castle that we decorated with bits of driftwood and sea grass, saving the prettiest seashells for the tops of the turrets. Then we waded into the chilly waters, leaping over waves and dancing away whenever someone spotted a crab—or *thought* she did! *Nothing could make today better than it is right now,* I thought happily.

But I had no idea what would happen that night.

We left the beach in the early afternoon so that there would be plenty of time to dress for dinner. Since Shannon and Clara were cooking up a storm, Nellie had to attend to Mom and me as well as Aunt Beth and Betsy. Even so, she found the time to fix my hair in an elegant style, with Mom's wedding stars twinkling like a tiara.

For my birthday dinner, we were joined by Nellie, Hank, Shannon, Clara, and David, which made for quite the party! I wished that it could have lasted forever, but all too soon, Nellie and Shannon started clearing the table.

"If you'll excuse me for a moment," Clara said as she rose.

Then, to my surprise, Betsy stood, too.

Aunt Beth was in on the secret—whatever it was.

Without saying a word, she started extinguishing the lights. I saw Mom and Dad exchange a smile. Whatever was going on, I seemed to be the only one in the dark.

Then I heard Betsy's clear, sweet voice begin to sing from the kitchen. One by one, everyone else at the table joined in, until they were all singing the "Happy Birthday" song to me! A moment later, Betsy appeared, carrying a layer cake with twelve candles flickering on top. Her smile glowed brighter than the candles as she placed the cake right in front of me.

"Make a wish, Kay!" she said.

I stared at the candles for a long moment, lost in thought. What on earth could I wish for? Surrounded by all the people I loved most in the world, I already had everything I could ever possibly need.

*I wish that the strength, love, and determination of Great-Great-Grandmother Katherine will always be with me.*

Then I closed my eyes and blew out the candles—all of them.

As everyone cheered, Shannon handed me a cake knife and said, "Would you like to do the honors, Miss Kay?"

"Certainly," I replied. The cake was covered in a thick layer of buttercream frosting, with a glossy layer of raspberry jam in the middle. There were even candied violets scattered across the top.

"This is delicious!" I exclaimed after my first bite.

"That's your cousin's doing," Clara said with a smile as she gestured at Betsy. "It was all her idea."

Betsy grinned back at her. "You know I would've been lost without you!" she said. Then she turned to me. "I asked Clara to help me make a birthday cake for you," she said. "You're so amazing, Kay; you can do anything! I'm quite hopeless in comparison. So I thought I'd learn how to make a cake for your birthday."

*So* that's *what Betsy and Clara have been up to,* I thought as relief flooded through me. *They weren't trying to avoid me. It was all part of the surprise!*

"Betsy's quite the determined baker. She wanted to do every step herself," Clara explained. "We picked raspberries and made them into jam. We even candied the violets!"

"We have a cake at home called a Victoria sponge," Betsy explained. "It's a lot like this, with a nice layer of raspberry jam in the middle. I hope you like it, Kay."

"I love it," I said as I took another bite. "The jam is the best part!"

Betsy and Clara exchanged a glance, then burst out laughing. "Kay, you wouldn't believe what a mess I nearly made of it," Betsy said through her giggles. "I thought I was measuring the sugar, but it was really the salt. Luckily, Clara noticed in the nick of time and saved me from spoiling it all!"

"That certainly would've been a memorable birthday cake," Dad teased her, and everyone laughed.

When we'd finished our cake, Betsy and Aunt Beth exchanged a glance.

"Now, Mum?" Betsy asked in a low voice.

"Yes, darling," Aunt Beth replied. "It's time."

"Beth," Mom said, shaking her head. "A birthday present, too? You've already been so generous to Kay—to all of us."

I squirmed a little in my seat. Besides a card, we hadn't been able to send anything to Betsy for her birthday. It felt awful that she and Aunt Beth had gone to the trouble to buy a present for me.

But when Betsy returned to the table carrying a small box, she walked right past me—and stopped at Mom.

"Here, Aunt Kate," she said. "This is for you."

*What's going on?* I wondered.

When Mom opened the box, a cry escaped her lips. She snapped the box closed and folded her hands over her face. Dad was by her side in an instant.

"Mom?" I exclaimed as I jumped up from the table. "Mom! What is it? What's wrong?"

But when she looked at me, I realized that Mom wasn't upset at all. Her face shone with a greater joy than I'd ever seen.

"Oh, Beth," she whispered. "How? How did you do it?"

"That's not important now," Aunt Beth said. "Go ahead, Kate. You know what to do."

Mom rose to stand beside me and took my hands in hers. She was trembling like a leaf—or maybe I was; it was hard to tell. *Is this it?* I wondered. *Will Mom finally tell me the big secret? Is it inside that box? But how did Betsy know before me? And why did Mom seem so surprised?*

"Sometimes in our lives, there are moments that we've always dreamed about," Mom began. "And sometimes there are moments that we didn't expect to happen. Right now, I'm experiencing both—at the same time."

I must have looked awfully confused, because Mom smiled at me and rested her hand on my cheek. "When we were interrupted yesterday, Kay, I was telling you about all the ways in which you remind me of Great-Grandmother Katherine. Your determination. Your resilience. And especially your loving heart. I wish that you and Katherine could've known each other, Kay. I think you would've gotten along famously.

"But even though Great-Grandmother Katherine is gone, in many ways, she's still with us," Mom continued. "Her remarkable life made ripples that still impact us—like the books you and Betsy found yesterday. There are so many ways, large and small, in which we can honor her memory. And this way, I think, would please her most of all."

Mom presented the small box to me. "Happy birthday, Kay, my dearest daughter."

As I struggled to unlatch the tarnished clasp on the box, I figured out which one of us was shaking.

It was me.

"I—I can't get this open—" I said.

"Here," Betsy said as she stood up. "Let me."

No one spoke as Betsy deftly slipped the tiny clasp out of its snug loop. Without opening the box, she returned it to me. I held my breath as I eased open the lid . . .

And saw the Katherine necklace sparkling up at me.

How could it be? It was gone—everyone knew it was gone—

Was I dreaming?

I looked wildly from Mom to Betsy to Aunt Beth to Mom again.

"What—how—" I struggled to speak.

And then I burst into tears.

In an instant, Mom and Betsy had wrapped their arms around me.

"Don't cry, Kay! It's your birthday!" Betsy whispered into my ear, but I could see tears shining in her eyes, too.

"Here, sweetheart," Mom said as she took the Katherine necklace out of its box. Then she draped the precious jewels around my neck and fastened the delicate clasp. The ruby-studded pendant rested lightly over my pounding heart; the gold was cool at first, but it soon grew as warm as my own skin.

"I thought I'd never get to wear it," I said. "I thought I'd never see it again!"

Mom kissed me and held my hand tightly, the way she used to when I was small. "Beth, *how*?" she asked. "How on earth did you do this?"

"We'd made arrangements to buy it from a man in London," Aunt Beth began.

"We traveled to the city the day before my birthday," Betsy interrupted. "But someone *else* had bought it, right out from under us! We were crushed, Aunt Kate! Absolutely crushed! We thought it was gone for good!"

"It made for a solemn trip home," Aunt Beth said. "But Betsy never wavered in her faith that we would someday find it again. And as it turned out, she was right. Because on her birthday, the very next day—"

Betsy clapped her hands. "You'll never believe it!" she cried. "Cousin Gabrielle burst into my room, first thing in the morning, with the Katherine necklace in her hand!"

"Cousin *Gabrielle*?" Mom exclaimed. She turned to Aunt Beth with a puzzled look on her face. "The same Cousin Gabrielle who nearly ruined *your* twelfth birthday?"

"The one and only," Aunt Beth said wryly. "She wanted to make amends for what she'd done so many years ago and had set her heart on giving the Katherine necklace to Betsy."

"I don't know why," Betsy spoke up. She reached into her pocket and withdrew—at last—the Elizabeth necklace. "I know you've been wondering where the Elizabeth necklace was, Kay. I made a promise that I wouldn't wear it until you had the Katherine necklace. It seemed too unkind to flaunt it in front of you."

"Oh, Betsy," I said, feeling a rush of love for my cousin. "You didn't have to do that. Seeing you without it was as wrong as me being without the Katherine necklace."

"I've been absolutely dying to tell you that we had the Katherine necklace," Betsy continued. "But Mum said we had to wait until the debt payment was made. Otherwise, the creditor could seize it from you. As long as we kept it in *our* possession, the Katherine necklace would be safe, as it technically belonged to us, not you."

My mouth dropped open. "What a difficult secret to keep!" I exclaimed.

"You have no idea," Betsy replied, shaking her head. "Mum and I had a terrible row about it on our first morning here because I wanted to give it to you straightaway. And that's why I insisted you pick out a red dress for the ball. Oh, Kay, your dress will look absolutely stunning with the Katherine necklace around your neck!"

*So* that's *what they were arguing about!* I realized with relief. *Betsy didn't want to leave early. She wanted to give me the Katherine necklace early!*

"Kay, let's promise right now to never keep another secret from each other. Families shouldn't have secrets. They're far too complicated," Betsy said.

"I promise," I replied. "But there's still one secret that we don't know."

Betsy knew exactly what I meant. She turned to her mother. "*Now* will you tell us the big Chatswood family secret?" she asked. "We've been *so* patient!"

Mom and Aunt Beth exchanged a mysterious smile. "Yes," Aunt Beth finally said. "Yes, I do believe it's time."

"And I think it's also time for us to bid you good

night," Shannon said as she rose from the table.

"But I want to find out the secret, too!" little David said before an enormous yawn muffled his words. Everyone started to laugh.

"It's off to bed with you, my boy," Hank said as he lifted David onto his shoulders. "Happy birthday, Miss Kay. The necklace looks as though it were made just for you."

Nellie embraced me, then Shannon. "I knew that the Katherine necklace would find its way home again," Shannon said.

Then Clara hugged me, too. "I'm so happy for you," she whispered in my ear.

"If you'll excuse me, I have some paperwork to attend to," Dad said with a knowing smile.

And suddenly the crowded room was nearly empty. Betsy and I moved closer together, and I reached for her hand. The moment was here: At last, we would finally, *finally* learn the secret that had haunted our family for generations.

"Should I begin?" Aunt Beth asked Mom, who nodded in response.

Aunt Beth turned to us. "You already know that

neither Elizabeth nor Katherine was eligible to inherit Chatswood Manor due to the strict inheritance laws in England," she told us. "Only a male heir could inherit the estate, which was why one twin would have to marry her cousin Maxwell Tynne."

"That's unfair," I said.

"*Terribly* unfair," Betsy added.

"Yes, it was," Aunt Beth agreed, "but the girls knew there was nothing they could do about it. They were bound by a deep sense of loyalty and duty; whichever one was chosen to marry Maxwell would do so without complaint."

"Sadly, their mother, Lady Mary, became ill when the twins were eleven," Mom said. "When it became clear that she would not recover, it was immensely important to her to know that her daughters' futures would be settled. After a great deal of consideration, she and your great-great-great-grandfather Robert decided that Elizabeth, the older twin, would marry Maxwell and eventually become the lady of Chatswood Manor. As a Chatswood daughter, Katherine would always be welcome in the great house, but she would be free to forge her own destiny."

"A *bit* more free," Aunt Beth said. "Robert would still choose her husband, as was the custom of the day. And he eventually selected Katherine's distant cousin Alfred Vandermeer, who was a good man, a *kind* man, and—most important to Robert—a wealthy man who would always be able to provide for his family."

*Yes, yes, we already know this,* I thought, trying to hide my impatience. I didn't want to wait one more second to find out the secret!

"There was just one problem, though," Mom said. "The heart is not as easily compelled as the mind."

I sat a little straighter; beside me, Betsy did the same.

"Elizabeth and Katherine well knew their duties and responsibilities to their family and to Chatswood Manor," Aunt Beth continued in a quiet voice. "But though Elizabeth was pledged to Maxwell—who, like Alfred, was a gentleman of the very highest regard— she knew that she could not love him. Not as long as she loved another."

"And Katherine had nothing but respect for Alfred," Mom said. "But that was all she felt for him. Katherine had no idea how she could ever marry a man she did not love—let alone make a life with him far away from her home and family."

"That's terrible," Betsy remarked.

"Just wait. There is so much more to the story," Aunt Beth told her. "The twins *had* fallen in love— but in the most inconvenient way. You see, Elizabeth and Alfred were deeply in love, while Katherine had secretly pledged her heart to Maxwell."

We were all quiet for a moment as Betsy and I absorbed the information. I felt a surge of pity for my great-great-grandmother and her sister. *How awful to marry someone you don't love . . . while your sister weds the man of your dreams!* I thought in dismay. If this was the family secret, I wasn't sure I wanted to know it anymore.

"But the girls—the young women, I should say— were optimistic," Mom said. "After all, they thought, as long as one of them married Maxwell, the conditions of the inheritance would be met. Chatswood Manor would stay in the family, and the other twin would be free to marry Alfred. And so they told their father about their predicament, expecting that Robert would understand and release them from their engagements."

There was a tone in Mom's voice—ominous,

dark—that made me suddenly nervous. Betsy's hand in mine was very cold.

"Unfortunately, he did not," Aunt Beth continued. "You must understand that Robert was from a different time entirely. All his life, he'd been told that it was his duty to make all the decisions—for the estate and for his family. He refused to be second-guessed, especially by his daughters. And so he denied their request."

"So Katherine and Alfred weren't in love?" I asked numbly.

Mom and Aunt Beth exchanged a glance. "No," Mom finally said. "Katherine never loved Alfred."

I sat back, stunned. How could that be? It felt like our entire family had been built on a lie.

"That's an ugly secret," Betsy said. "I wish you hadn't told me."

"Or me," I added.

"Wait, my dears," Aunt Beth said. "We're not at the secret yet."

"You mean there's still *more*?" I asked.

"As their eighteenth birthdays—and their wedding days—approached, the twins were in turmoil," Mom said. "Neither could imagine marrying a man she didn't love. And so, true to their natures, they took matters into their own hands. Katherine and Elizabeth Chatswood switched identities."

The room was completely silent. I don't think any of us even dared to breathe.

"Elizabeth became Katherine, and Katherine became Elizabeth," Aunt Beth finally said. "Remember, only their mother could truly tell them apart, and she'd been dead for six years. They switched everything— their wardrobes, their hairstyles, their names. Their destinies."

"Almost everything," Mom corrected her. "The one thing that neither girl could bear to part with was her necklace. And so, as Katherine changed her name to Elizabeth, her sapphire necklace changed its name, too, and became the Elizabeth necklace."

"The reverse was true for Elizabeth and her ruby necklace," Aunt Beth said, gesturing to the Katherine necklace I was wearing.

"And that is the long-held secret of the Chatswood and Vandermeer families," Mom concluded. "A secret kept for generations, known only by a few people . . . and now, Kay and Betsy, you."

I was too astonished to speak. So Great-Great Grandmother Katherine had been born . . . *Elizabeth*? In another world, in another life, she could've stayed in her homeland and become the lady of Chatswood Manor. I would've been born in England, not America. *My* name would be Betsy—Lady Betsy—not Kay.

*No, it wouldn't,* I told myself. *Because if Katherine— Elizabeth—my great-great-grandmother, hadn't married Great-Great-Grandfather Alfred, I wouldn't even be here.*

My fingers fluttered to the ruby necklace dangling around my neck. Rubies that were as red as fire and as hard as rock; rubies that would not ever tarnish or fade. They would glitter for me just as they had for my great-great-grandmother and for every woman who had worn the Katherine necklace since her. I could only hope and pray that these everlasting rubies would give me a fraction of the strength my great-great-grandmother had shown when she had walked away from her old life, becoming a new person in a new world—and all for love.

"How sad," I said suddenly. "How sad and lonely to give up your name, so that no one would ever know who you really were."

"But also romantic," added Betsy, and I had to agree. I could scarcely comprehend all that our great-great-grandmothers had done in the name of love. Would there someday be an event as romantic in my own life?

"We'll never know the toll the switch took on Elizabeth and Katherine," Mom began, "but I do know that they both considered it a very small price to pay to follow their hearts, and that their lives were rich in joy and love, blessings to which we should all aspire."

"But *someone* must've known." Betsy suddenly spoke up, a frown wrinkling her forehead. "Surely they told *someone* their secret, or else how would you know?"

Mom and Aunt Beth smiled together. "Their husbands knew, of course," Mom said. "And they confided in Essie Bridges after they wed. And then, to the best of our knowledge, neither Elizabeth nor Katherine spoke of it again until July sixth, 1914."

I knew that date. "Your birthday?" I asked Mom.

She nodded. "My twelfth birthday, to be exact," she said. "What a day that was! Beth had left abruptly that morning, and I was heartsick to think that it would be years before I might see her again. I'd been presented to society at my birthday ball and had snuck into the East

Wing for the very first time—where I'd discovered, of all things, a letter that Great-Great-Grandmother Mary had written to Elizabeth. I couldn't begin to understand how Elizabeth's letter had journeyed all the way to America, when she was never able to make the trip. I'd even met Essie Bridges, who'd been living secretly in the East Wing. I was filled to the brim with questions! And Great-Grandmother Katherine was ready to answer them."

"Your mother wrote to me that very night," Aunt Beth said. "When I read her letter, which arrived the very next day after I returned home to Chatswood, my shock was so great that I nearly fainted!"

"I think it was a relief for Great-Grandmother Katherine, frankly," Mom said. "She had held that secret in her heart for decades. How freeing it must've been to finally confide in someone else. When she heard Aunt Beth and me join our necklaces together, it brought back so many memories of her youth and her beloved sister that Great-Grandmother Katherine could no longer hide the truth."

"When I think about this secret, as I often have over the years," Aunt Beth began, "I'm struck by Katherine and Elizabeth's devotion. Not only to their own happiness, but to each other. To me, there is no stronger testament to the power of family."

Betsy turned to me, holding out the Elizabeth necklace. I knew what she wanted to do before she said a word.

I lifted my necklace to hers and we slid the half-heart pendants together until they were joined as one. *Click-click-whirrrrrrr.* The metallic gears inside the heart were almost inaudible, until an unseen door in the back of the pendants sprang open.

"Katherine and Elizabeth's secret message is still in there," Mom said. "Aunt Beth and I replaced the letters when I attended her wedding in England."

"'A part of you forever,'" Aunt Beth recited. Then she smiled at us. "We added our own message, too."

Betsy and I leaned our heads close together as we peered inside the hidden compartment. In addition to the yellowed snips of paper containing Katherine and Elizabeth's message, there were two miniature scrolls. Betsy plucked them out with the tips of her fingers and handed one to me. Though I had to squint to read the impossibly tiny letters, I recognized my mother's handwriting immediately.

"Cousins by blood," Betsy read from her scroll.

"Sisters by heart," I read from mine.

"As true now as it was then," Aunt Beth said as she put her arm around Mom's shoulders. "Perhaps you two will have to think of your own message to add before Betsy and I go home."

From the way Betsy and I smiled at each other, I knew that that was exactly what we would do.

*T*hat night, no matter how hard I tried, I couldn't fall asleep. I couldn't stop thinking about everything that had happened—the delightful birthday dinner; the stunning return of the Katherine necklace; and most of all, learning the astonishing secret that my great-great-grandmother had held so close to her heart.

Early in the morning, as the sun was beginning to rise, I sat up in bed and wrapped my arms around my knees. *I wish I could've known her,* I thought, feeling especially sad that Great-Great-Grandmother Katherine had died before I was born. There was so much I wanted to ask her; so much I longed to say about her sacrifices and her bravery—but she was gone forever.

Or was she?

Mom always said that she felt close to Great-Great-Grandmother Katherine in her rooms in Vandermeer

Manor; that was why Mom had never dismantled them. Maybe I could visit Katherine's rooms right now—this very night!

Without making a sound, I climbed out of bed and took my flashlight out of my bedside table. Then I pulled on my bathrobe and slippers before I tiptoed out of the room. I didn't want to wake anyone so early, especially after the night we had had. Mom kept a spare set of keys to Vandermeer Manor in the drawer of the telephone stand; they winked at me as they reflected the sunrise spilling through the windows.

I opened the door and stepped out into the cool, clear morning. I could hear the lonely echo of waves crashing on the shore. I started running through the dewy grass toward Vandermeer Manor, my heart thundering in my chest. *I'll just go for a few minutes*, I told myself. *No one will even know that I left.*

Instead of entering through the grand front doors, I hurried to the back of the house, where there was an old wooden door hidden by a curtain of ivy. Almost nobody knew about this little-used entrance to the East Wing, but it was the fastest way to get to Great-Great-Grandmother Katherine's rooms. The skeleton key fit perfectly in the tarnished lock; a half turn and the door swung open. It was that easy to get inside.

The flashlight's beam was dim and wobbly, but it was enough to guide my steps. I moved quickly through Essie Bridges's old rooms, pausing just once at the bookcase where I'd discovered the valuable Charles Dickens books. A smile crept across my face. *Thank you, Great-Great-Grandmother Katherine,* I thought.

Inside Katherine's room, I turned on the tiny light on her desk. There was something sacred about this place, where all of Great-Great-Grandmother Katherine's possessions lay exactly as they had when she was alive. I breathed in deeply. Was that her gardenia-scented perfume I could smell, still hanging in the air?

I ran my finger along the polished edge of the mahogany writing desk, imagining all the letters Katherine had written to Elizabeth there. Then I peeked inside one of the drawers and found a leather-bound agenda with 1917 stamped on the cover in gold ink. *Her last datebook,* I realized, remembering that she had died in January 1918. I turned each page slowly as I marveled at the details of Great-Great-Grandmother Katherine's days, written in her own hand.

*February 1917: BBS meeting. Kathy most effective as chairwoman. A pleasant afternoon.*

*April 6, 1917: Painted in the garden. Essie's young friend visited. Brought her much joy!*

*June 30, 1917: Kate chaired another meeting of Bridgeport's Red Cross chapter. The girls rolled enough bandages to outfit a hospital! So proud of my great-granddaughter.*

Sometime in August, the daily entries became weekly; and then there was nothing written for two months. *She was slowing down,* I realized sadly.

*November 29, 1917: Thankful that Alfie is too young to fight in this dreadful war.*

After I read the last entry, I wandered over to a

narrow bookcase. It was crowded with dozens of books, including several slim volumes in worn leather covers. They had to be very old. *As You Like It . . . The Tempest . . . A Midsummer Night's Dream . . .*

*William Shakespeare's plays*, I thought, smiling to myself as I pulled *All's Well That Ends Well* off the shelf. *It looks like a complete set. If only they'd been initialed by the author, too!*

I'm not sure what made me check inside the front cover. I didn't really expect to find *W.S.* scrawled there by a quill pen.

I definitely didn't expect to find the same *C.D.* that was written in the Charles Dickens books, though.

A frown crossed my face. *That's strange,* I thought. *Why would Dickens have initialed these books? That doesn't make any sense.*

Unless . . . he hadn't initialed the other books, either.

Unless . . . we'd made a terrible mistake.

I brought several books over to the desk so that I could examine them in better light. In each one, I found the same initials, no matter who the author was. With every book I opened, my doubt grew.

Slowly, as if in a dream, I reached for Great-Great-Grandmother Katherine's agenda. I scanned the pages quickly, checking each entry for capital letters. The *C*, I had to admit, was a definite match for my great-great-grandmother's handwriting. But her *D*'s didn't match at all.

Then I spotted one of her *L*'s.

It was identical. Great-Great-Grandmother Katherine's *L*'s were so loopy that one could be mistaken for a *D*.

*C.L.*, I thought numbly. *Chatswood . . . Chatswood . . . Chatswood library.*

I groaned. It all made sense now, in the worst way. Before leaving Chatswood Manor, Great-Great-Grandmother Katherine had taken some of her favorite books from the library and packed them among her things. *What better reminder of home*, I thought, *than a favorite book you've read again and again?* Perhaps she'd meant to send them back. Or perhaps she'd simply wanted to always remember where they came from. Either way, there was no doubt in my mind that she'd written the initials *C.L.* in each book that she'd brought with her from the Chatswood library.

Which meant that the Dickens books we'd sold to the man at POB Enterprises were certainly not worth a fraction of what the buyer had paid for them. The money that Mom and Dad had used to pay off the debt was based on a lie.

It had never been our intention to swindle him.

But that was exactly what we'd done.

*If I tell,* I thought anxiously, *if I tell . . .*

The investor might want his money back.

Mom and Dad might default on the debt.

And I might have to part with the Katherine necklace to make it right—this time for good.

9

The terrible secret lay heavily on my heart as I closed up Vandermeer Manor and walked through the morning mist with Great-Great-Grandmother Katherine's datebook and one of the Shakespeare plays tucked under my arm. Back in my room, I crawled into bed, tucking the datebook and the play beneath my pillow for safekeeping. Then I cupped the Katherine necklace in my hands. *Great-Great-Grandmother Katherine*, I wondered, *what would* you *do?*

But I already knew the answer to that, didn't I?

At some point I must've fallen asleep, because the next thing I knew, bright, midmorning sunlight was streaming in the window, though Betsy, for once, was still sleeping. I blinked my eyes a few times. Had last night—had my entire birthday—been a dream? It was hard to believe everything that had happened was real.

But there was the Katherine necklace hanging around my neck, sparkling in the sun.

And—I reached under my pillow—there were the books I'd taken from Great-Great-Grandmother Katherine's room.

A deep sense of acceptance—of peace—settled over me as I held the datebook to my chest. I knew what I had to do.

"Good morning, Kay," Betsy said in a sleepy voice. "What's that?"

"Good morning," I replied, only a little surprised by how calm my voice sounded. "It's, well—I'll tell you in a minute. Hurry up and get dressed. I've got to talk to Mom . . . and you and Aunt Beth should be there, too."

Betsy's eyes opened wide. "Now you've got my attention," she said as she threw back her blankets.

A few minutes later, we found Mom and Aunt Beth sitting in the kitchen, enjoying their morning tea.

"Good morning, girls. You two are up early," Mom remarked.

"I have something to show you," I said.

I put the datebook and the play on the table. And

I told her everything. No one spoke as first Mom, then Aunt Beth, and finally Betsy compared the initials in the play to the writing in the datebook.

"Yes," Mom finally said. "I'm inclined to agree with you, Kay. I do think this is Great-Grandmother Katherine's handwriting. Your theory about the initials standing for Chatswood library is as likely as anything else I can think of."

"What are you going to do?" Aunt Beth asked bluntly.

Mom put her hands in the air, palms up. "What can I do?" she asked. "What choice do I have? I'll call Vivian and tell her that we made a mistake."

"The buyer didn't care if the initials were verified, though," Aunt Beth pointed out. "Surely he knew he was taking a risk by insisting on such a fast sale."

"That's true," Mom replied. "But if he really didn't care, he won't ask for his money back. Disclosing this information is the right thing to do."

"It's so disappointing," Betsy said in a quiet voice. "I really thought that everything was going to work out so well."

Mom smiled wistfully at her. "So did I," she said.

"But this is just another bump in the road. Say, that gives me an idea. Why don't I ask Vivian to set up a meeting with POB Enterprises in New York? Then we can explain the situation to him face-to-face. If he does want his money back, we'll have to move faster than we expected, since Dad already paid off the debt in full. We'll . . . I don't know, accelerate the sale of the town house or—or—"

"Let's cross that bridge if we come to it," Aunt Beth said, placing her hand over Mom's. "Go ahead and call Vivian, and we'll start getting ready for our trip."

I followed Mom into the entryway. Before she picked up the phone, I touched her arm. "I'm sorry, Mom," I said.

"For what, sweetheart?" she asked. "You did absolutely the right thing. Alfie's shady dealings and dishonest practices led to the trouble we're in now with Vandermeer Steel. Your father and I are determined that its recovery will not chart the same course."

"If I'd kept it a secret—"

"No," Mom interrupted me, shaking her head. "I'm proud of you. And I know that Great-Grandmother Katherine would've been, too. Now, run along and find

Shannon, and ask her to come see me at once."

"Yes, Mom," I replied. Then I hurried off to Hank and Shannon's cottage. I had to knock three times before Shannon came to the door, disheveled and flustered, with Clara behind her.

"I'm sorry," I said. "Am I interrupting?"

Clara opened her mouth to answer, but Shannon spoke instead. "Not at all, Miss Kay. What can we do for you?"

"Mom would like to see you right away," I said, still looking at Clara, who wouldn't meet my eye.

"Of course," Shannon said as she stepped outside, pulling the door shut behind her. By the time we got home, Mom was just hanging up the phone.

"Kay, Shannon, excellent," Mom said, beckoning us into the living room. "We've got a lot to do and very little time. Shannon, we'll be traveling to New York tomorrow on the first train."

Shannon began scribbling furiously in her little notebook.

"I expect we'll be there for two or three days—maybe four," Mom continued. "We'll stay with Kathy and Katie at the townhouse, of course. So a traveling suit, three day dresses, and perhaps one evening dress for each of us ought to suffice. If you and Nellie could help us pack today and, of course, accompany us—"

"Mrs. Kate, I apologize for interrupting," Shannon finally said. "It would be my pleasure to help you and Miss Kay get ready for your trip. But if it's all the same to you, might Nellie attend you in my place?"

Mom raised her eyebrows in surprise. "Of course, Shannon. Is everything all right? You always enjoy a trip to New York City."

Shannon nodded, smiling. Were those tears shining in her eyes? "Forgive me, Mrs. Kate. I'm a bit sentimental this morning. You see, my Clara has decided to take a position as lady's maid to Mrs. Morgan in Boston!"

*No!* I thought in dismay.

"Oh, Shannon!" Mom exclaimed. "Was this expected? I always thought that Clara wanted employment at Vandermeer Steel."

"The offer came a few days ago," Shannon explained. "I didn't mention it because Clara was so dead set against it. But last night, she changed her mind."

Shannon paused to look at Betsy and me. "I think it was what you did to bring the Katherine necklace

home, Lady Betsy," she said. "Last night, Clara said—
she said, 'Mum, I'm ready to do my part.' And I tell
you, Mrs. Kate, it was like she'd finished her growing
up right before my very eyes."

"You must be so proud of her," Mom said. "As we
all are! Yes, Shannon, of course you must stay to help
Clara get ready for her big move. When does her new
position start?"

"Sooner than I'd like," Shannon admitted. "Mrs.
Morgan wants her to begin in less than a week! It will
be a mad flurry to get everything ready in time, but I
think we're up for the challenge."

"Of course you are," Mom said firmly. "Now, I want
you to draw up a list of anything that Clara needs
before she moves to Boston. We won't be able to give
her the send-off she deserves, but Joe and I want to do
something special for her before she goes."

"And so do I," I said, speaking for the first time
since I'd heard the news. I smiled as broadly as I could,
but a deep sadness was settling inside my heart. Clara
would be gone in less than a week, and Betsy a few
weeks after that.

Life would be very lonely without the two of them.

We left before dawn the next day, crowded into the back of the car with our trunks while Dad drove us to Providence to catch the earliest train to New York City. Dad gave me an extra-big hug before we boarded the train. If he was worried about the outcome of our meeting with the buyer for POB Enterprises, he didn't show it.

Shannon had packed some blueberry muffins for us to eat on the train, but I was so sleepy that I kept yawning between bites. I'm not sure who fell asleep first, but Betsy and I didn't wake up until we arrived at Pennsylvania Station, right in the heart of New York City. After we got off the train, Aunt Beth stood very close to us, with her hands on our shoulders, while Nellie saw about our luggage and Mom found us a taxicab. I was glad that Aunt Beth was there. Even though I'd been to New York City before, the frenzied bustle of the big city always took me by surprise.

Mom appeared then, adjusting her hat as Nellie and a porter wheeled our trunks behind her. "I think I've gotten everything settled," she said. "There's a taxi waiting for us at the curb. Hurry! I don't want him to find another fare before we get there!"

Luckily, the taxi was still waiting right where she'd left it, and the courteous driver maneuvered through the crowded streets to bring us to the Vandermeer brownstone on Park Avenue.

"Here we are, ladies," the driver announced. "May I carry your trunks inside for you?"

"Yes, please, that would be greatly appreciated," Aunt Beth replied as she fumbled in her change purse for the fare. Suddenly, the door beside me opened with a *whoosh.*

It was Aunt Katie and Great-Aunt Kathy! They were really my great-aunt and great-great-aunt, but they insisted I call them by the same names as Mom did. I grinned when I saw them there—Great-Aunt Kathy looking as dignified as ever with her ivory-tipped cane and ostrich-plume hat, and Aunt Katie wearing a dove-gray dress the exact color of her hair. They'd been in New York for three weeks already, and I'd missed them every day.

"Oh my dears, my dears!" Great-Aunt Kathy cried as we climbed out of the taxi. "You've arrived!"

"We're ever so glad to see you!" Aunt Katie exclaimed as she kissed my cheeks. "Happy belated birthday, Kay!" Then she turned to Betsy and held out her arms for a hug. "And what a pleasure to meet you, Betsy. Kate told us all that you and your mother did to recover the Katherine necklace. We'll forever be in your debt."

Betsy ducked her head shyly. "It was the least we could do," she replied.

Aunt Beth stepped forward. "I'm so glad to see you both again," she said as she kissed my aunts.

While Aunt Katie showed the driver where to leave the trunks, the rest of us sat in the parlor, which had been stripped of nearly all its furnishings. Only a few chairs and a lamp remained.

"You *have* been busy!" Mom remarked as she glanced around the bare room.

"We were grieved to miss your birthday, Kay,"

Great-Aunt Kathy told me. "It was very considerate of you to bring the celebration to us instead."

"We've ordered a cake from François," Aunt Katie said excitedly. "Now, Kate, you mustn't scold us. We had a bit of money and we thought, what better use than to make a little party?"

"I wouldn't scold you," Mom said with a gentle smile.

"There is so much to celebrate," Great-Aunt Kathy said. "And, of course, we hope to be home in time for the grand birthday ball in a few weeks."

*Celebrate?* I thought. *What on earth does she mean?* We were on the verge of losing every cent we'd earned from selling the books—and perhaps the Katherine necklace, too. Celebrating was the last thing we should do.

My confusion must've been obvious, because Great-Aunt Kathy reached for my hand. "I can see you disagree, little Kay," she said. "But you've got to look at the situation from a different angle. A new perspective is as easy to try on as a new hat, you know. Tell her what we have to celebrate, Katie. Go on."

"Well, Kay's twelfth birthday, of course," Aunt Katie began, ticking each reason off on her fingers.

"Seeing dear Beth and meeting the lovely Betsy. The chance to bid our New York home a fond farewell. And, of course, the return of the Katherine necklace, when we thought we'd never see it again."

"Come here, child," Great-Aunt Kathy said, holding a wrinkled hand out to me. "Let me take a closer look."

I obediently crossed the room and stood before her. She nodded approvingly, a wistful smile on her face.

"You know it's been decades since I wore the Katherine necklace, and it hasn't lost a bit of its sparkle," she declared. "It suits you well, Kay. How glad I am to see you wearing it."

"So you've had a nice time in the city?" Mom asked. "I was worried that it would be too much work for you—"

"Too much work? For us?" Aunt Katie asked, sounding surprised.

"Nonsense!" Great-Aunt Kathy said with a laugh. "We've had a grand time of it—oh, there were so many glorious memories made in these rooms over the years! Katie and I could've succumbed to the doldrums, I suppose, as we sorted through everything—*oh, this is the doorway where John hung the mistletoe; oh, this is the piano where Eleanor played "Auld Lang Syne" every New Year's*—but really, I must say that it's been a gift to be here one last time before the sale."

"I think we both agree that we'd rather say good-bye to it all now than to have never had it in the first place," added Aunt Katie. "And we'll always have those lovely memories. No one can take those from us."

My fingers pressed the Katherine necklace against my chest. I was painfully aware that I might have to say good-bye to it soon—perhaps tomorrow, even. But Aunt Katie was right. No one could take away my memory of wearing it, and that was a gift I never thought I'd have.

"What time is your dinner?" Great-Aunt Kathy asked suddenly.

"Half-past five," Mom replied.

Great-Aunt Kathy glanced at her timepiece. "You've just enough time to bathe and dress, I'd say," she remarked. "Especially with just one lady's maid to attend you all."

"I do hope your meeting is a success," Aunt Katie said . . . but there was sadness in her eyes that told me she was prepared for the worst.

"Keep your chin up," Great-Aunt Kathy advised us. "No matter how it turns out, we'll all have cake together on the balcony afterward, and stay up as late as we please. There's always something to look forward to."

A few hours later, Betsy, Aunt Beth, Mom, and I stood outside the entrance to the Waldorf Astoria, a grand hotel not far from the Vandermeer brownstone. Buoyed by Aunt Katie and Great-Aunt Kathy, I'd felt like I could do anything. But now, the thought of meeting the collector behind POB Enterprises and explaining the truth about the books filled me with anxiety. I wanted to keep it all—the debt repayment, the shares of Vandermeer Steel, and the sense of security that had lightened our hearts.

And especially the Katherine necklace.

*How much did Great-Great-Grandmother Katherine lose?* I asked myself. *What did she leave behind forever? And all to follow her heart.*

Somewhere, buried under all the things that were so easy to want, the truth shone brighter than a beacon. We'd have those things—the money, the stocks, the security, even the Katherine necklace—fair and square, or we wouldn't have them at all. And so it was with my head held high that I walked into the Waldorf Astoria.

"Good evening," Mom said to the maître d'. "Vandermeer, party of five."

"Yes, madam," he said. "Your dinner companion has already arrived. I took the liberty of showing him to your table."

"Wonderful," Mom said with a charming smile. I walked behind her as the maître d' led us to our table, wishing that I could be half as collected as she was. Then Betsy fell into step beside me and linked her pinky finger with mine, and I felt better right away.

"Your table, madams," the maître d' announced.

The gentleman at the table rose and turned around to face us.

I recognized him right away—and, strangely enough, so did everyone else. My mouth dropped open in amazement. Never in my wildest dreams did I expect to meet him—let alone have dinner with him at the Waldorf Astoria!

"It's—it's—it's Paul O. Brady!" I exclaimed.

"Paddy!" cried Mom, beaming.

"Patrick O'Brien?" gasped Beth and Aunt Betsy.

$\mathscr{P}$aul O. Brady, the famous movie director, smiled at us—the same dazzling smile that I'd seen in every copy of *Hollywood Hello*. "What a pleasure to see you all," he said—as though he knew who we were!

To my surprise, Mom walked right up to him and took his hands. "Paddy, how long has it been?" she asked warmly. "Fifteen years?"

"A little more than that, Mrs. Wilson," he replied.

"Please, call me Kate," Mom told him.

I turned to Mom. "You *know* him?" I exclaimed. "You *know* Paul O. Brady?"

"Excuse me." Aunt Beth spoke up. "I'm sorry to interrupt, but what exactly is going on? Betsy and I know this man to be Patrick O'Brien. We met him in London last month at the botched sale of the Katherine necklace."

The smile on Mom's face began to fade, replaced by a look of confusion.

Mr. Brady—or whoever he was—held up his hands. "I can see I've got a lot of explaining to do," he began.

"I should say so," Aunt Beth said. She was perfectly polite, yet there was an icy edge to her voice that gave me chills. "I would be grateful to hear more about your obvious interest in the Vandermeer family, as well as learn why you have so many different identities."

"That's fair," Mr. Brady said pleasantly. He pulled out a chair beside him. "Lady Beth, would you care to have a seat?"

Aunt Beth hesitated for a moment before she sat. The rest of us followed.

"Lady Beth is correct—my real name is Patrick O'Brien," Mr. Brady—I mean Mr. O'Brien—began. "Kate here knows me as Paddy, because that was my nickname when we met many years ago, right after I emigrated from Ireland in 1916."

"Yes, it *was* 1916," Mom suddenly remembered. "I was holding all those Red Cross meetings at the house, rolling bandages for the war effort. I'd see you coming and going from the East Wing when you visited Essie."

"Essie Bridges was my great-aunt," Mr. O'Brien said in a quiet voice.

One look at the faces around the table showed me that everyone else was as surprised as I was.

"You see, my great-grandfather was a man named Sean O'Brien," Mr. O'Brien continued. "Shortly after he married, he went to India for work, and his bride, Maggie, took a position as a housemaid at Chatswood Manor until he could return. Sadly, Maggie died giving birth to their daughter, Essie, and the midwife didn't know how to contact my great-grandfather. As a girl, Essie knew nothing about her parentage. When she was old enough, she, too, sought employment at Chatswood Manor—where she was hired as a ladies' maid to Lady Elizabeth and Lady Katherine.

"But my great-grandfather never stopped looking for his wife," Mr. O'Brien said after a pause. "Eventually, his search led him to Chatswood Manor. Maggie's fate would've remained a mystery if not for the efforts of two young girls who were determined to discover the truth. Thanks to Lady Katherine and Lady Elizabeth, my great-grandfather was not only able to find out what had happened to his dear wife, but to meet Essie, the daughter he didn't know he had."

"No one ever told me that part of the story," Mom said softly, and Aunt Beth nodded in agreement.

"To finally know what had happened to his wife, to find out that he had a daughter—it meant everything to my great-grandfather," Mr. Brady said. "After he moved back to Ireland, he eventually married again and had more children—but he never lost contact with his first child, Essie. Not even when she moved all the way to America with Lady Katherine. The bond they shared filled a hole in each of them. And all thanks to the Chatswood twins."

"What a touching story," Mom said.

"I'm still a bit confused," Aunt Beth said, though her voice was warmer now.

"Bear with me. I know it's complicated," Mr. O'Brien said apologetically. "After Great-Grandfather Sean died, all of us kids in Ireland stayed in touch with our far-off aunt Essie. My sisters married, one by one, and then there was me—the baby of the family—with very few prospects. There was war on the Continent and rebellion in Ireland. In early 1916, Aunt Essie wrote to me. 'Come to America,' her letter said. 'Come without delay. This great country can become your home, as it did mine.' And in the envelope was enough money to pay for passage across the Atlantic Ocean. It was an opportunity I'd never dreamed I would have. How could I pass it up?"

Mr. O'Brien swallowed hard before he spoke again. "Of course, I knew full well where the money came from. It came from the same woman who let me stay in the East Wing of Vandermeer Manor with my aunt until I could find lodging of my own. The same woman who noticed my threadbare clothes and gave me a fine suit that had belonged to her late husband. The same woman who made one phone call and had me hired at Vandermeer Steel. The very same woman who'd helped Aunt Essie find her father all those years ago."

"Great-Great-Grandmother Katherine," I whispered.

"That's right," Mr. O'Brien said, nodding. "Even back then, I knew that I'd be forever grateful for everything that Mrs. Vandermeer had done for me—from the new suit to the new job to the new life. And most of all, for the chance to get to know my aunt before she died. I visited with Aunt Essie whenever I wasn't working. We'd talk for hours about work and the weather, about our faraway family, about my wildest dreams and her sweetest memories. Sometimes I'd go see a picture show and tell her all about it afterward, and one evening I confided in her my biggest secret: that I wanted to direct a movie myself one day. And do you know what she did?"

We all waited, breathless, for the answer.

"She pulled out this old wooden box and opened it with a Celtic-knot key—I just knew it was something she'd kept from the old country—and she handed me a stack of money. 'You go to Hollywood, Paddy,' Aunt Essie said. 'You go tomorrow and you make your motion pictures. You've got great stories in you, my boy, and if you don't tell them, who will?'"

Then Mr. O'Brien looked right at me. "So you see, Miss Kay, that you're right as well. I did indeed become a movie director. There was quite a bit of bad feeling toward the Irish back then, so I decided to use Paul O. Brady as my professional name."

"*Across the Way* is my favorite movie!" I exclaimed. "You're the best director who ever lived!"

"That's high praise, Miss Kay, but any success I've had came from what your family did for me," he replied earnestly. "Everything I am—everything I've become—is a direct result of the kindness and generosity of the Chatswoods and the Vandermeers."

"Mr. O'Brien, this is an amazing story," Aunt Beth said. She nearly sputtered with disbelief. It was all so much to take in. "But how does it relate to the Katherine necklace and the Dickens books?"

"Aunt Essie died, and shortly thereafter, Mrs. Vandermeer," Mr. O'Brien said. "I hardly knew Kate, so my ties with the Vandermeers were severed. But not a day passed that I didn't remember how much I owed them, my very life included—for how would Sean O'Brien have been able to marry again and start a new family if Lady Elizabeth and Lady Katherine hadn't helped him uncover the truth about his first wife? I've followed your doings over the years; I'm sure you know that you're a regular feature in the society pages, here and abroad. When I read about your troubles in the papers, Kate, it gnawed at me. I wanted to help you more than anything—really, it was the least I could do. But I knew you'd balk at accepting anything from me, a veritable stranger."

"You're quite right there," Aunt Beth said wryly,

making us all laugh. "Heaven knows, I've tried."

Mr. O'Brien leaned forward. "Then I had this idea, you see," he continued. "I remembered all the priceless antiques in Vandermeer Manor, and I thought, if their need should grow so great that they start selling their belongings, I'll be there to buy them."

"POB Enterprises!" I exclaimed suddenly, putting it all together.

"Smart girl," Mr. O'Brien said approvingly. "I sent notices to all the antique dealers on the Eastern Seaboard to let them know that whatever the Vandermeer family might sell, I wanted to buy. Of course, I don't consider myself the owner of any of it. More like the . . . caretaker. I've been keeping it safe for you."

I reached up to touch the Katherine necklace. *Keeping it safe*, I thought, as a wave of gratitude washed over me.

Mr. O'Brien must've noticed, because a smile crossed his face. "I recognized the Katherine necklace as soon as I heard about it," he said. "You'll have to tell me how it made it home again, because I was heartsick when I accidentally sold it to the wrong person. Especially knowing that it was the last possession

Elizabeth kept when she became Katherine."

A ripple of shock passed around the table. *He knows!* I thought. *Mr. O'Brien knows the secret!*

"I'm so sorry—is that still a secret?" he asked in alarm. "Essie told me—I thought surely you knew—"

"Oh, we did," Aunt Beth assured him quickly. "I think we're all just a bit surprised that *you* knew!"

"Paddy—Patrick—I don't know where to begin," Mom said. "You've been like a guardian angel to us. How on earth will we ever be able to thank you?"

"Thank *me*?" he asked in surprise. "Kate, you've got it all wrong. I owe everything to your family. I'll never be able to thank *you*."

"There is something I have to tell you, though," Mom said.

I knew exactly what she was going to say. *Here it comes*, I thought. *The moment of truth.*

"It's about the Dickens volumes," Mom continued. "Some new information has come to light proving that they weren't initialed by Dickens after all. I'm afraid you've grossly overpaid for them. I am, of course, more than willing to refund your money, but it will take a day or two to—"

Mr. O'Brien laughed suddenly, catching us all off guard. "Dickens? You think I cared about Dickens's initials?" he asked in a kind way. "Gracious, no. I wanted those books so badly because I used to read them to Aunt Essie. Those hours we spent sitting side by side, the smile of happiness on her face as I read . . . *A Christmas Carol* was her favorite. . . . Overpaid? On the contrary. Those books are precious to me, at any price."

It took me a moment to understand exactly what Mr. O'Brien meant. When it dawned on me, it felt like the clouds had parted, letting in the most glorious sunlight. *He doesn't want the money back!* I thought joyfully. *We won't have to sell the Katherine necklace!*

Mom was so overcome with emotion that she had trouble speaking. When at last she found her words, they were simple . . . and enough. "Thank you," she said, again and again. "Thank you."

"Now, listen, there was another reason why I accepted your invitation to meet today," Mr. O'Brien said. "I have a proposition to make."

I sat a little straighter in my chair. There was something about the intensity in his face that made me believe the next few moments could change everything.

"The history of the Chatswoods and the Vandermeers is a story for the ages," Mr. O'Brien declared. "Secrets ... mysteries ... drama ... intrigue ... and most of all, *love*. It's got all the ingredients of a runaway hit. Now, if you'd consider selling the rights to your story to POB Enterprises, I know that we could surely make a fantastic movie. And a lot of money, too."

"Sell the rights?" Mom asked.

"To our family history?" Aunt Beth added. They stared at each other across the table, a long look that was impossible to read.

"You don't have to answer right away," Mr. O'Brien said quickly. "We're prepared to be *extremely* generous with the terms. You'll have full approval over the script, which I'll write myself. And, of course, I'd want to shoot on location, at Vandermeer Manor and Chatswood Manor. If I may, I'm confident that you'd make enough from this picture to buy back control of your company ... and then some. So take some time; think it over—"

"Yes," Mom and Aunt Beth interrupted him, speaking at the same time.

"Yes?" he repeated in surprise. "You'll do it?"

"Yes!" Mom said as happy tears filled her eyes. "It sounds like a phenomenal opportunity. We'd be fools to pass it up!"

"And the time for secrets has passed," added Aunt Beth. She placed her hand lightly on Mr. O'Brien's arm. "I think that Great-Grandmother Elizabeth and Great-Aunt Katherine would be so pleased to hear how they influenced your remarkable life, Mr. O'Brien. To honor them in a movie is a tribute they never could've imagined. Thank you."

"You must come to Vandermeer Manor at your earliest convenience," Mom said to Mr. O'Brien. "We have so many materials you can use in your research."

"Nothing would please me more," he said . . . but he was still looking at Aunt Beth.

The waiter appeared then to bring us our menus, but I didn't think I could eat a single bite. There was so much to do. . . . Call Dad with the good news . . . tell Aunt Katie and Great-Aunt Kathy that we wouldn't have to sell the town house after all . . . and, most of all, let Clara know that she could turn down the job in Boston. After all, Vandermeer Steel would be back in my family's control soon, and I already knew that we would need talented mathematicians in the accounting office.

I leaned toward my cousin. "Betsy, can you imagine it?" I whispered. "Our family story brought to life on the silver screen! We'll be famous! Who do you think will play us?"

"Paulette Lyons?" she said, giggling. "Annabelle Edwards?"

"And did you hear what else he said?" I continued. "He wants to shoot on location at our homes!"

"You *must* visit when he films at Chatswood Manor!" Betsy exclaimed.

Suddenly, I remembered what Great-Aunt Kathy had said that afternoon: *There's always something to look forward to.*

From Betsy's and my twelfth birthday ball . . .

To visiting, at last, Chatswood Manor—the place where it all began . . .

To a movie about our families . . .

The future had never looked brighter!

# EPILOGUE

You go first—"

"No, you—"

"No, *you*—"

"Shhh," Shannon whispered to us, one finger at her mouth. "When the music stops, there will be complete silence in the ballroom. The guests mustn't hear you giggling before your debut."

Shannon's gentle advice was all it took for Betsy and me to stop playing around. We stood there as quiet and prim as portraits while Shannon and Nellie circled around us, adjusting the skirts of our ball gowns and fluffing our hair. But when it came to positioning our necklaces so that they caught the light *just so*, Betsy and I turned to face each other.

"There," I said, moving her sapphire necklace a little to the left.

"Just right," she said as she centered the ruby pendant over my heart.

Shannon stood back to examine us both. "Perfect," she finally said—and just in the nick of time, because the words were barely out of her mouth when the music suddenly stopped.

It had all seemed like fun and games a moment ago, but when I realized that Betsy and I were about to descend the grand staircase into the ballroom, I felt like my heart might stop. Betsy's eyes were wide as they searched my face; she looked as nervous as me.

"Together," she mouthed without making a sound, and I nodded with relief.

We paused for a moment at the top of the staircase, glancing at each other out of the corners of our eyes. Seeing my beautiful cousin beside me was all it took to make my nerves fade away. How special it was—how right in every way—to share this moment with her.

Then, arm in arm, we began our descent—just like our great-great-grandmothers had at their birthday ball in Chatswood Manor, more than eighty-five years ago.

*Mom walked these steps before her birthday ball,* I

thought. *And Aunt Katie before her, and Great-Aunt Kathy before her . . .*

They were waiting for us at the bottom of the steps, of course; first Dad and Mom; then Aunt Beth; then Aunt Katie and Great-Aunt Kathy. Then came Betsy's cousin Gabrielle, all the way from Paris, and half the lords and ladies of England. Senator Hebert and his wife stood next to the foreman from Vandermeer Steel and his wife, who were followed by all the employees of Vandermeer Steel, including the company's newest hire: Clara. Shannon and Nellie must've run all the way down the back staircase, because they were standing on Clara's other side, with Hank and David, too. And—yes, there was Mr. O'Brien, standing right behind Aunt Beth. They seemed to be spending a lot of time together these days.

I looked out at the sea of smiling faces. It was a rare and wonderful thing to have everyone who'd ever mattered to me together in the same room at the same time. *Never forget this moment,* I thought.

It was thirty-seven steps to the ballroom—Betsy and I had counted the day before—and it felt like it took an hour to walk down them all. I think it must've gone much faster than that, though, because the next thing I knew, the music had started up again, and one person after another approached to wish us happy birthday. Then came the dancing—hours and hours of dancing!—until Betsy and I were so pink in the face that we had to pause for some refreshment. We stood against the wall, sipping our punch and whispering behind our gloved hands.

"Look!" I said, nudging her with my arm. "They're dancing *again*."

Betsy glanced in the direction of her mother and Mr. O'Brien. She shook her head, but couldn't help smiling. "That's the *fifth* time they've danced together tonight," she said.

"Quite scandalous, don't you think?" I teased her.

"Do you know what she said to me yesterday?" Betsy asked. "She asked if I'd ever fancy taking a trip to Hollywood!"

I gasped. "Really?"

"I said, 'Only if Kay can come, too,'" Betsy replied.

"I wouldn't miss it for the world!"

"Speaking of missing . . . ," Betsy said, glancing around the ballroom. "Do you think anyone would notice if we slipped away for a few moments?"

"Now?" I asked. "I guess there's no time like the present."

Betsy and I were completely dignified as we left the ballroom. But as soon as we were out of sight, we started to run—and we didn't stop until we'd reached Great-Great-Grandmother Katherine's rooms.

"Did anyone see us?" I asked breathlessly.

Betsy shook her head. "I don't think so," she replied. "But we'd better be quick about it. If we're not back in time to cut the cake . . ."

"I know."

Sitting in the center of Great-Great-Grandmother Katherine's writing desk was the journal that had belonged to Essie Bridges so long ago—the one that Aunt Beth had found in the secret passageway of Chatswood Manor. I'd hidden the journal in Katherine's rooms that morning, with something very special tucked inside the cover. I opened it and removed a miniscule piece of paper.

Then I turned to face my cousin.

At the same time, we held up our necklaces.

"I am Kay, and I love my cousin Betsy."

"I am Betsy, and I love my cousin Kay."

*Click-click-whirrrrrrr.*

When the hidden door in the back of each necklace popped open, Betsy and I peeked inside. It was getting a little crowded in there with all the letters—*A P-A-R-T O-F Y-O-U F-O-R-E-V-E-R*—and the two messages our mothers had added before we were born:

*cousin of my blood*

*sister of my heart*

But there was still enough room for one more secret.

I handed the piece of paper to Betsy and watched her unfold it. "Well?" I asked anxiously. "Is it all right?"

For a moment, she didn't speak. Then Betsy looked up at me, all smiles. "It's better than all right!" she cried. "It's perfect!"

I beamed at her. "We can tear it right down the middle—"

Betsy clapped her hand over my drawing. "No, I'd hate to rip it—"

"It's fine. I'll make another. Come on, Betsy. You know we have to. One half for your necklace and one half for mine."

"If you insist—but I can't watch!"

I folded the paper in half and made a neat tear right down the center of the Chatswood-Vandermeer family tree I'd drawn. "There! All done," I told her.

Betsy uncovered her eyes. "Oh, good," she said in relief. "It's not ruined."

"Not at all," I said.

Then Betsy tucked the Vandermeer half of the family tree inside her necklace, while I hid the Chatswood side in mine. Together, we pressed the tiny door closed; then we pulled our necklaces apart.

The Katherine necklace didn't feel any heavier with the Chatswood branch of the family tree hidden inside it, which made perfect sense to me. All those names I'd written in my tiniest handwriting—from Elizabeth to Eliza to Liz to Beth to Betsy—were my family as much as Katherine and Kathy and Katie and Kate were. Their stories already lived within my heart. I would always carry their strength and love with me, through good times and bad, no matter what.

And that was no secret.

*Ready for new secrets?*

Read on for a first look at a
new family with secrets
all their own in
Camille's Story,
1910

*I* stared into the pot as the water began to boil, melting the knob of butter into a shiny yellow slick. "Now?" I asked anxiously. "Should I add the flour now?"

Across the kitchen Mama was whisking egg whites at a furious pace. "Is the butter melted, Camille?" she called.

"Almost," I replied. "Almost . . . yes!"

"Good. Now add the flour all at once and stir as hard as you can. Mind the stove now. I don't want you to burn yourself again."

"All at once?" I repeated.

"Yes, just pour it in and begin stirring. Don't stop until it's come together in a thick dough."

"Yes, Mama."

I bit my tongue as I reached for the flour; Mama

had helped me measure just the right amount. *All at once*, I reminded myself. Then I poured the flour into the pot. But I must've poured it a bit *too* fast, because a huge cloud of the stuff rose into the air!

"Oh!" I cried, rubbing my powdery face. *"Ah-ah-ahhhh-choo!"*

The scullery maids started to giggle—and who could blame them? My shenanigans at the stove were a constant source of entertainment for the entire kitchen staff. But I knew that they didn't mean any harm by their laughter. After all, I'm sure I made a funny picture, now that my dark, chestnut-brown hair was as white as a powdered wig!

"Are you all right, Camille?" Mama said. "Keep stirring!"

"Yes, Mama, I'm fine," I replied as I tried not to sneeze again. I focused all my attention on stirring, stirring, stirring the gooey mix in the pot. Mama was a fine pastry chef who had been trained by her father, the famous chef Alistair Beaudin, who was known throughout all of France for his delicious desserts. The Beaudin family method for making light, delicate profiteroles was a carefully guarded secret, and just one of the reasons why Monsieur Henri and Madame Colette Rousseau had been so eager to hire Mama when she finished her apprenticeship. Mama had been just as eager to accept their offer of employment, since she and my father, the groundskeeper at Rousseau Manor, were engaged to be married. Monsieur Henri used to joke about what a perfect match it was, bringing together two sweethearts and satisfying his sweet tooth at the same time. But he had stopped making that joke after Papa died.

Mama and I still missed Papa terribly, but Monsieur Henri and Madame Colette had done everything in their power to ease our pain. Since they had no children, the Rousseaus had dedicated their ample time and fortune to helping others, including Mama and me. Just after Papa's death, the Rousseaus had promised that they would always take care of us, no matter what. And in keeping that promise, they had earned our loyalty—for life. It was a privilege to work at Rousseau Manor, one of the grandest homes in all of France. The manor, and the estate it sat on, had been in the Rousseau family for generations. Ever since my tenth birthday almost two years ago, Mama had been trying her best to train me in the pastry arts so that I, too, could carry on the Beaudin family tradition. But despite my heritage, I was a disaster in the kitchen! Somehow, though, Mama had limitless patience with me. And if she wouldn't give up, then I wouldn't, either.

I stirred and stirred until my arm began to ache. Then, like magic, it happened: the sticky flour and buttery water combined to make a smooth, shiny dough.

"Mama!" I cried. "I did it! I did it!"

"Well done, Camille!" she said proudly from across the kitchen, and even the scullery maids began to applaud. I beamed with pleasure.

"Now what?" I asked.

"Let it rest for a few minutes to cool," Mama told me. "Then you can add the eggs, one at a time. Twelve ought to do it. Remember to beat well after each addition, Camille. And don't add them too soon, or else the heat from the dough will cook them."

"I won't," I promised her. Then I ducked into the pantry for the eggs I'd gathered that morning. Since spring had arrived, the hens had been laying even more eggs than usual; I'd already collected two large baskets and it wasn't even noon! I wouldn't be a bit surprised if

Mrs. Plourde, the cook, decided to make a quiche for luncheon.

I held out my apron skirt to make a pouch for the eggs as I counted them, one by one. As I gently placed each egg in my apron skirt, I heard a sharp voice say my name. My heart sank. I knew who it was right away: Bernadette, the head housemaid, and one of the most powerful servants at Rousseau Manor. Bernadette was quick to find fault, especially with me. She was always displeased with how I folded the napkins or scoured the pans. Even my thick hair, which resisted all my efforts to stay in a tidy plait, seemed to offend her.

"Camille!" she barked again. "What are you doing?"

"I was—"

"Dawdling, most likely," she spoke over me with a contemptuous sniff. "As if there wasn't enough work to be done around here."

"But—"

"No excuses," Bernadette said as she grabbed hold of my elbow and escorted me back to the kitchen. "Now, show me your task, or I'll send you off to polish the silver."

"I'm making dough for the profiteroles," I tried to

explain as I carefully placed the eggs in a bowl. "There's croquembouche on the menu tonight."

"Croquembouche?" Bernadette asked. She raised an eyebrow in disbelief. "And your mother trusted you with the profiteroles?"

I nodded miserably. It was no secret that croquembouche, a tall tower made of airy profiteroles filled with creamy custard and held in place by a sticky caramel sauce, was one of the most challenging desserts to make. Even I had to wonder what Mama was thinking when she asked for my help.

"Then you'd best get on with it," said Bernadette. She folded her bony arms across her chest, and I could tell that she intended to watch every single thing I did.

*What if the dough is still too hot?* I worried. I snuck a glance around the kitchen, but Mama must have stepped out.

"Get on with it, I said," Bernadette snapped.

# sewzoey

If you love the gorgeous gowns
in Secrets of the Manor,
wait until you meet Zoey Webber,
a seventh-grade fashion designer!
Check out the Sew Zoey books,
available at your favorite store!